THE COWGIRL CODE

QUEENS OF MONTANA, BOOK 1

VANESSA GRAY BARTAL

DRY CREEK PRESS

PROLOGUE

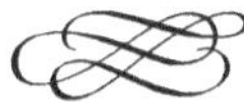

"There are four of them, the poor little things."

Anne heard the nurse speaking and knew she was talking about her family. She glanced at her sisters to make sure they were asleep. They were.

"Do they realize she's dying?" another nurse asked the first one.

"I think the oldest two do," the other nurse said.

"How old is the oldest?" the second nurse asked.

"Twelve. They're all two years apart, and they're all named after royalty. She told me before she slipped into a coma."

The second nurse clucked her tongue in sympathy. "What about the father?"

"Haven't you seen him?" the first nurse said, and her tone turned dreamy. "He's a cowboy. He owns some big ranch in the middle of nowhere. He's hardly spoken two words to anyone since they've been here. He's the strong silent type."

"Poor little dears," the second nurse said. "To be so young and lose their mother to cancer." She clucked her tongue again.

"That oldest one is going to have to be mother to all of them now," the first nurse said.

"She's tiny for twelve; she looks more like ten. That's too much responsibility for one so young. She'll never be able to mother those three other girls." The topic moved on to other patients, but Anne tuned them out.

She turned to look at her little sister, Libby, sitting beside her on the uncomfortable bench in the hospital's waiting room. Libby had each of their two younger sisters tucked under her arms and cuddled against her side. At ten Libby had already started taking over the household duties such as cooking and cleaning, but even more than that she was a born nurturer. She had always liked to play house and dolls and dress up in fancy, frilly outfits. She was like a mother hen to eight year old Kitty and six year old Maggie. No, Anne wouldn't have to become a mother to her siblings; Libby would take care of that. She thought of her father and the haunted, distant look that had been in his eyes the past few days since their mother's death became imminent. He was closing up and pulling away from them. Already he had started to forget to do important things around the ranch, like order feed and immunize the new calves. Anne had to remind him, and when he still didn't do it she did it herself. No, she wouldn't become the mother in this family; she would become the father. She would pick up the slack to make sure they didn't lose the ranch. She would provide for her sisters and help her father cope. She sat up straight and dried the tears that had been unobtrusively coursing down her cheeks. She wasn't a little girl anymore. In fact, she couldn't act like a girl any more at all. She had to be strong and take care of this family. From now on she was the head of this household, and they were all her responsibility.

CHAPTER 1

Will Ashley stepped off the train and stretched. The feeling that he was traveling back in time had grown with every mile he logged on his westward journey. It was the twenty first century; who still used trains for transportation? Anyone who came to this part of Montana, apparently. The nearest train station was an hour away from the ranch by car.

He opened his phone to call his mother but put it away. There was no signal. He would have to wait until he reached his destination to call. He hoped they had a phone, and not one of those old-fashioned versions that ran on a party line and required a crank.

It was when he shoved his phone in his pocket that he first saw the boy. He was noticeable because he was a local: a real, live cowboy. He wore a white Stetson, a western plaid shirt, dark jeans, and well-worn cowboy boots.

Will's fellow train occupants stared at the boy as if he were part of a show, and no wonder. It was clear by their comfortable clothing, luggage, and cameras they were tourists. Their stares made the boy angry and he worked his face into a mutinous scowl. Will was as oddly fascinated by the boy as the tourists. Was he a cowboy? If so, why was he at the train station in the middle of the day? There was something intriguing about him that made Will wonder what his story was.

A large van arrived to pick up the group of tourists. The van had the markings of a local ranch. Will had the smug thought that he would be having the same experience as the tourists, only he would be getting paid for it.

He moved to lean against the bricks of the train depot. This position gave him a better view of the interesting boy while he waited for his ride to appear.

The boy grew more tense and agitated by the second. Without moving his feet he peered into the train as if willing someone to appear. When the train started to move and no more passengers emerged the boy whipped off his hat, threw it to the ground, and yelled, "Tarnation!"

At that point Will realized two things: First, the word "tarnation" was still in use. He had been under the impression the expression became extinct in the eighteen hundreds. Second, and most important, the boy wasn't a boy at all; he was a girl. When the hat came off a thick bundle of long brown hair cascaded down her back.

"I'm sorry," she said softly.

Will opened his mouth to tell her there was no need to apologize when he realized she was talking to the hat. She bent over, picked it up, and lovingly dusted it off.

She whirled to face Will, and then stopped, clearly startled. "Oh," she said, and her mouth froze open in that position. She stared at Will as he stared at her.

Something about the girl captured Will's interest. Maybe it was the surprise at learning she wasn't a boy. Maybe it was because her pretty mouth was puckered into a silent vowel. Maybe it was because for one split second her big brown eyes were unguarded and he could read longing and sadness in them as clearly as if they had been a book. Whatever the reason, he wanted to talk to her, to learn more about her.

"Can I help you?" he asked politely. "You seem upset."

Her eyes became guarded again, and she knocked her hat against her leg. A puff of dust erupted from the contact. "Not unless you're a busybody old lady named Ashley."

A note of alarm rang in Will's ears. "I'm a busybody young man named Ashley."

The girl stared at him as they shared the same thought. "I'm supposed to pick up a lady named Ashley Will."

"I'm Will Ashley," he said slowly, and things started to click into place for him. "Do you work for Mr. Chapman?"

The girl nodded. "He's not going to be happy."

Will blew out a breath. "I imagine not. Why don't you take me to him and he and I will discuss it?"

Now she blew out a breath. "He's driving cattle and won't be home for three days." She shifted her weight from foot to foot and ran a hand tiredly over her face. "Now what?" She bit it out angrily and then raised her hat as if about to dash it to the ground again.

Will caught her wrist before she could throw the hat. "You wouldn't want to have to apologize to it again, would you?"

She wrenched her wrist out of his grasp, but a smile tugged at the corners of her mouth. "Come on, Ashley," she said, and turned her back to him. "I guess I can't leave you here."

They collected his bags and he followed her to the truck. It bothered him more than a little that she carried the two heaviest bags, but she was deaf to his protests.

"What is it you do for Mr. Chapman?" Will asked once he was seated inside the pickup truck.

"You won't need it," the girl said as she noticed his search for a seatbelt. "There aren't any other cars or trees. If we crash you'll land in a field of soft wheat." She smiled, either at her joke or the mental image.

"Your job," he prompted.

"I'm the foreman of the ranch."

Will laughed before realizing she was serious. She shot him a look that could melt the paint off a building.

"But you're," he started, and she interrupted him.

"I'm what? A woman?" Her grip tightened on the steering wheel.

He laughed again and clapped his hand over his mouth. He was clearly offending her, but she was tiny, and even covered in dirt and dust she was cute. "I was going to say young. How old are you?"

"Eighteen," she answered defiantly. "How old are you?" Her tone held a challenge he didn't understand.

"I'm twenty."

She nodded curtly. "And how did you get this job? What did you tell Mr. Chapman about yourself?"

"Nothing," Will said. "I saw the job in the paper and sent him my resume. He hired me as soon as he read it."

She let out a frustrated sigh. "Figures. What did the job posting say *exactly*?" She turned to look at him and her eyes dared him to lie to her. He almost laughed at her again but held himself in check. She was just so *cute*.

"It said, 'Wanted: A man to spend the summer on a Montana cattle ranch caring for and tutoring four little girls.'"

She banged her palm repeatedly and forcefully on the steering wheel. "It was supposed to say woman. Didn't you wonder why someone would hire a man to watch four little girls?" She turned accusing eyes to him.

"Of course I did," he answered defensively. He and his mother had talked about this very thing. "It's one of the reasons I took the job. I was concerned for their safety. I knew I was a trustworthy choice, but what if he got someone who wasn't?" He paused and frowned at her. "I'm relieved to hear the ad was wrong. It worried me about what kind of father would intentionally hire a man to watch over his little daughters. Do you know the little girls?"

"Yes," she said shortly.

"What are they like?"

"Indescribable," she said, and another smile twitched her lips.

"Are they well behaved?"

"Depends on your definition." She glanced at him and her eyes sparkled with repressed amusement. "Don't take this personally, Ashley, but I don't think you'll be there long enough to find out much about them. The situation is obviously impossible." She smiled and the effect was intoxicating to him.

"You don't like me," he guessed.

"I don't know you," she replied in a somewhat softer tone. "I don't like the idea of you."

"What's your idea of me?"

"A busybody spy come here to boss the girls and disrupt our lives." Her frown returned.

"And what is it to you? If you're the ranch foreman why do you care?" he asked.

"Because everything that goes on at the ranch is my business and because the girls are my responsibility. *I* watch over them, and no one else."

"What about their father?" he asked.

"He's busy," she bit out.

"What about their mother?"

"She's dead," she said softly, and then threw on the brakes, put her hands over her face, and started to cry.

For a split second Will didn't know what to do. With any other girl he knew how to handle tears. In fact it was one of the things he did best. This girl was different. She was all prickles and edges. Still, she was a woman. There had to be a soft heart in there somewhere.

He slid across the seat and gathered her to him. To his surprise and delight she melted into his embrace. She pressed her face to his chest while her hands clung to his shirt. She cried for a long time, great, heaving, gulping sobs. He got the impression she had been storing it up for months, or maybe years. He wished he knew her name so he could use it to try and comfort her. As it was, he ran a gentle hand down the back of her head over and over until her tears finally spent themselves, and even then she still didn't let him go. She kept her face firmly pressed against him until a tense awareness of each other crept between them. She moved away from him slightly and peered up into his face.

Her big brown eyes were like melted chocolate and her lashes were wet. Tears had left dust trails on her cheeks, and her lips still quivered.

"What's your name?" he whispered.

"Anne." She whispered, too.

"Annie," he repeated, and it worked to clear her out of her trance.

She shoved away from him, hard. "No, not Annie, Anne. Don't ever call me Annie." She threw the truck into gear and took off.

He nodded and looked out his window to hide his smile. She had tried to inject anger and force into her words, but he knew the truth now. Somewhere under her hardened exterior she was sweet, soft, and warm.

Annie, he thought, *you and I are about to become very good friends.*

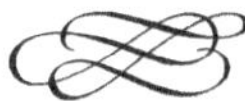

CHAPTER 2

It took an hour to drive to the ranch. After her crying jag Anne glared through the windshield and refused to say another word, despite the fact that Will peppered her with questions. Finally they arrived at the sprawling ranch house. Anne disembarked the tall truck, grabbed Will's bags, and headed inside. Will grabbed his remaining bag and followed her.

A pretty teenager in a flowing yellow dress came to the door to greet them. She stopped short at the sight of Will, smiled at him, and then looked around him.

"Where is she?" she asked hesitantly, as if afraid of the answer.

"This is her," Anne said, and indicated Will with a wave of her hand.

The other girl looked at Will and smiled again. "Eastern women are handsome."

Will laughed, and Anne rolled her eyes. "Stop flirting and go get the girls."

The girl turned away and bounded off.

"Come on," Anne said shortly. She led Will to a spacious bedroom with its own bathroom. "You'll have to settle in later. We have business to tend to." She spun on her heel and left the room. He understood he was to follow her.

By the time they arrived in the living room the first girl had returned along with two more teenagers in tow. Anne gave the other three girls a look and they sat meekly on the couch.

"This is Elizabeth," Anne introduced the girl in the flowing dress. "We call her Libby. She's sixteen. This is Katherine." She pointed to a studious-looking girl with braces, glasses, and short dark brown hair. "We call her Kitty. She's fourteen. This is Margaret." Margaret was wearing a t-shirt and cut-off denim shorts. She was covered in more dirt than Anne was, and she was holding a frog. "We call her Maggie. She's twelve."

Will inspected the four girls with curiosity while they inspected him. "You live here with the Chapman girls?" he asked. Something wasn't right, but he couldn't place his finger on what it was.

"We are the Chapman girls," Anne replied in a flat tone.

"The ad said you were little girls."

Anne clenched her fists and her jaw. "My father thinks we are," she replied tightly. She turned back to her sisters. "Which one of you changed the ad?"

Libby and Kitty looked confused. Maggie squirmed uncomfortably and focused on her frog.

"Maggie," Anne said harshly, and Maggie jumped. "Why?"

"You said it was going to be awful. You said she would make us follow rules and tell us what to do." Maggie swallowed hard. "You said she might try to marry Dad and be our mom."

Anne pressed her palms to her eyes. "Maggie, what are we supposed to do with him?" She jerked her head at Will. "He thought he had a summer job. He's going to have to go back home and miss out on weeks of work, not to mention Dad is going to be furious, and I'm the one who's going to be blamed."

"I'm sorry," Maggie whispered. She stared to cry. "I'm sorry," she repeated, and then ran out of the house.

Anne let out a breath. "Libby, see that he settles in and gets some food. Kitty, don't pester him with questions until he's had a chance to rest." With that she turned and exited the house.

Will studied the two remaining girls. The one called Kitty looked less like a Kitty than anyone he had ever seen. She was inspecting him as if he were a slide under a microscope. Libby was looking at him, too, but in a way that was far more disconcerting.

"What should we call you?" she asked, and her voice was as gentle and feminine as her manner.

"Will," he said, and then looked around. "Where did Annie go?"

Kitty and Libby laughed. "Better not let her hear you use that name," Kitty said. "She hates it."

"Our secret," Will said, and then gave them a smile.

"Anne went to work," Libby volunteered. "Come into the kitchen and I'll make you a snack."

"What does Anne do?" he asked as he took a seat at the kitchen table.

"Everything," Libby answered. "Except cook and take care of the house. I do that." She set two muffins and a glass of milk before him.

"What do the other girls do?"

"They have a few chores, but that's it. Anne and I want them to be little girls as long as they can. She would probably do more in the house to try and keep me from doing it, except she knows I enjoy it so she lets me."

He bit into a muffin. "These are delicious," he said when he could talk, and he meant it. They were homemade and not from a mix. "You should go to culinary school. In Pittsburgh we have a Le Cordon Bleu cooking school."

Libby sat at the table and rested her head in her hand. "Interesting. How old are you?"

"Twenty."

"Hmm." She sighed dreamily. "Do you have a girlfriend?"

"Sort of, and even if I didn't you are too young for me, and you're technically in my charge, at least for the moment. So get any impure thoughts out of your pretty little head, Miss Libby." He smiled to take any sting out of his words.

"Well, that's no fun."

His smile widened. "I think I'll take a little walk. I sat for a long time today. Thank you for the snack." He stood and walked outside. He wouldn't admit even to himself he was looking for Anne.

His eyes scanned the vast horizon. He saw a female form huddled by a stream, but he knew it wasn't Anne; it was Maggie. He made his way over and sat beside her.

"Hey," he said softly.

"Hey," she sniffled. She was still crying.

"Do you own that frog, or are you borrowing him from nature?"

"Borrowing," she said, and gave a ghost of a smile.

"May I see him?" She nodded and handed the creature to him. He turned it on its back and rubbed its belly a few times.

"It fell asleep," Maggie exclaimed.

Will smiled. "Want me to wake him up? I know the magic words."

Maggie nodded enthusiastically.

"Wake up, frog, or Maggie is going to kiss you and turn you into a prince." He turned the frog over and Maggie gasped when it opened its eyes.

"How did you do that?"

"Who wants to be a prince? I scared him so bad he woke up."

Maggie giggled and set the frog in the water. "I'm sorry I ruined your life." She started to cry again.

"Are you kidding me? I'm having an adventure. I've never been to Montana before," Will said.

"My dad is going to be mad at me." She put her hands over her face and cried in earnest.

"No he won't, I won't let him," Will said. He scooted close and put an arm around Maggie's shoulders. As if she had been waiting for comfort she turned and threw herself into his embrace.

Maybe it wasn't a mistake, Will thought as he held a second member of this family while she cried. *Maybe I was sent here for a purpose.*

For the next hour he played with Maggie in the creek. Any minute he expected her to become bored and suggest they watch television, but she was absorbed by looking for crawdads, and then delighted when she found one. He couldn't help but notice the contrast between Maggie and his cousin Hillary, who was the same age. Hillary dressed like a college student and was never without a cell phone in her hand. She could text while doing anything, almost like a bizarre talent. Maggie, on the other hand, was wearing two long braids down either side of her head, no makeup, and clothes that looked like they belonged to a little boy in the nineteen forties. Despite the fact that Will had been raised to find Hillary's brand of preteen as normal, he preferred the way Maggie was innocent and untouched. The way a little girl should be.

"Do you have a cell phone?" he asked, and she dropped the night crawler she had been holding.

"Nah. It wouldn't do much good. The nearest tower is over an hour away at the Henshaw's."

"The Henshaw's?" he asked.

"Our nearest neighbors to the east." She pointed toward what was presumably the east.

His eyebrows shot up. "Your nearest neighbors are an hour away?"

She nodded. "By car. As the crow flies, or by horse, it's more like half an hour or so. They're the richest people around and Mr. Henshaw had a cell tower built on his land so his hands could use phones to talk to each other. They own a helicopter, too." Her eyes were wide and excited, and he could imagine the gossip the wealthy family evoked.

"Do you get television reception?" Will asked.

"No, but Dad bought satellite a while back, and we have the Internet, too, although Kitty says it's slow compared to everyone else on the planet."

He chuckled at that and turned over another rock.

CHAPTER 3

*A*nne watched them surreptitiously from the barn. She told herself it was because Will Ashley was a stranger and shouldn't be left alone with her guileless little sister, but it wasn't the whole truth. He was compelling in a way she wouldn't have suspected.

She always thought if she met an easterner, one who was from the city no less, that he would be repulsive to her. He would be weak, afraid of his own shadow, and condescending toward her country ways. Instead this stranger seemed self-assured and slightly in awe of ranch life. There was also something in his eyes, something she hadn't seen since her mother's death, something like tenderness.

But men couldn't feel such soft emotion, could they? She had certainly never seen it in a man before. Her father cared about her, she knew, but he showed it by providing for her and her sisters and teaching them what they needed to know to survive. He certainly didn't say it, but that was normal, wasn't it? Above all he wasn't comfortable with crying, but this strange man had seemed unfazed by her embarrassing tears. In fact, he had almost looked like he wouldn't mind joining her out of sympathy. She wrinkled her nose. If there was one thing she knew it was that men didn't cry. Ever. Not when calves kicked them and broke their bones, not when beloved dogs were mangled by coyotes, and not even when their wives died.

In a way she was almost sad her father was going to send the new boy away as soon as he learned of the mistake. It would have been interesting to get to know him and compare him to the other men she knew, purely as a scientific study. She was sure he would come up lacking in every way. He wasn't as handsome as some of the brawny cowboys she knew, but there was something appealing about him with his thatch of light brown hair and big brown eyes. His looks were reminiscent of her own, she thought. People could probably mistake them for relatives except she was short and petite and he was tall and broad-shouldered.

He paused mid-sentence with Maggie and looked toward the barn, almost as if he sensed her presence, but that was impossible. She was completely hidden. Or was she? She stepped farther back into the shadows. He dropped his eyes back to Maggie. After a few more minutes they went inside and Anne turned distractedly to her work.

As soon as Will entered the house Libby handed him a cool glass of iced tea. He hadn't realized he was parched until he held the drink in his hand.

"Thanks," he said, studying Libby while he sipped it. She was a lovely girl and an obvious nurturer. Right away, he had felt a connection to her, but it was lacking any romantic undertone. He wondered why that was. Previously, she would have been his usual type: sweet, pretty, and feminine. Maybe it was because she was four years younger and in his care. More likely, he admitted, it was because her older sister already held his attention.

Kitty, the next eldest in the family after Libby, sat at the table and studied him as if he were a curiosity in a museum exhibit. He remembered Anne's exhortation for her to wait until he settled in before she asked any questions.

"Was there something you wanted to ask me, Kitty?"

"If you don't mind," she said gently.

"Fire away," he said, and she did. Her questions weren't what he was expecting, and they were odd for a fourteen year old girl. First she asked about the history of Pittsburgh, his home town, and then she wanted specifications on the type of train he had traveled on to get there, and then she gave him a trigonometry problem that had been plaguing her. He was thankful math was his strong suit and he was able to solve it with minimal effort.

"You girls are interesting," he commented.

Kitty gave him the studying look again. "That means we're weird when you say it like that."

He smiled. "Not weird; charming. You're not like the other girls I know, and that's a compliment." They were quirky, but he liked quirky.

"Blame our mother," Kitty said. "She named each of us after a British queen. She was a history buff, and she wanted each of us to be strong and independent, or so I'm told. I don't remember much." Her gaze dropped to the table.

"Tell me about the British queens," Will said as a way to steer the conversation to a lighter topic.

Kitty's face lit. She loved sharing knowledge with willing subjects. "Anne was named for Anne Boleyn, the second wife of Henry VIII and mother of Elizabeth I. That's the Elizabeth Libby is named after. I'm named for Katherine Howard, Henry's first wife, the one he sent away when he met Anne. Maggie is Margaret Anjou, the wife of Henry VI. The one thing all of them have in common is that they all ruled alone at one time, either because they never married or because their husbands were ill or out of the country. I for one am hoping my fate turns out better than my namesake's." She gave him a wry smile.

"Undoubtedly it will," he said. "Just stay away from fickle and rotund royalty."

She stood. "Uh, oh, I'd better cancel my date for Friday."

Will and Libby laughed as she exited the room.

"That brings up an intriguing question," Will said as casually as he could manage. "Who do you date living way out here in the country?"

Libby spoke over her shoulder while she kneaded and shaped a mound of bread dough. "There's no one. The only eligible male for miles around is Marcus Henshaw, but he's your age, and as you pointed out that's too old for me."

But not too old for Anne, Will thought. Was she dating this Henshaw person? "What about your ranch hands?"

She paused and wrinkled her nose at him. "Cowboys aren't for me."

But what about for Anne? He couldn't figure out a way to ask without tipping his hand. Maybe he already had because she was giving him a speculative look.

"These are strange questions for a tutor to be asking."

"I'm fascinated by all aspects of the ranch. It's different from my life." That was true enough. Coming here was like stepping into a different world, not only because it was like something from a bygone era, but also because it was outside the realm of anything he had ever experienced. He had an inkling the rules were different here, and he would need to tread carefully until he learned them. If he stayed, that is, and he wanted to stay very much. The more he got to know the family, the more he sensed they needed him. There was something sad and disconnected about them, and he wanted to help. Also, if he were being honest, he wasn't ready to leave Anne yet. She was a mystery he was dying to solve.

That night at supper it was Will's turn to feel like an object of fascination. All the girls except Anne stared at him with rapt attention as if at any moment he might attempt a moon landing. Anne never once looked up from her food. The three younger girls' frank appraisal amused and unnerved him.

"This food is delicious, Libby," he said. He couldn't believe someone so young could cook so well.

"You must cook."

This came from Anne, and she said it with such certainty as she glanced at him that he was vaguely insulted.

"Why must I?" he asked.

"Because none of the men I know can cook," she said and returned her attention to her food.

"What does that mean?" he asked. He could feel his temper starting to rise.

"It seems like the sort of thing," she paused and tried to think of the right word, "a sensitive man would do."

"And what is wrong with cooking or being sensitive?" A frown now felt etched on his face.

"So many things are wrong with it that I wouldn't know where to begin," she said. The other three girls were now bouncing their attention between Anne and Will like spectators at Wimbledon.

"So you're telling me that someday when you get married and you're sick, you will be insulted and repulsed if your husband takes care of you and cooks supper for you?" he asked.

Libby, Kitty and Maggie laughed and put their hands over their mouths when Anne gave them a quelling glare. There was some inside joke he wasn't aware of.

"I don't get sick," Anne said. She settled her focus on her food as if the discussion were over.

"What about when you have a baby? You'll need help then. Don't you want your husband to help you?" he asked. He wasn't sure why he couldn't let this go, but it seemed imperative to keep going.

She paused and blushed, quite prettily, he thought. "Why would I want my husband to take time out of his busy work to wait on me hand and foot?"

"Don't you want him to share your life with you completely? To be there when you're sick and when you're well? To hold you and love you and care about you?"

Her scowl deepened, but the other girls were looking at him with wistful, dreamy expressions. Anne noticed, and it notched up her temper even more. "Oh, quit," she snapped at them. "Real men don't fawn over their women like lovesick puppies. Real men do what needs to be done. They provide for their families by working hard. They're strong, always."

"I agree with you," Will said, and her eyebrows rose in surprise.

"Only I think our definitions of strong are different. I think it takes strength to be able to show and tell people how much you love them. It takes strength to come home from a long day of work and take care of your wife and kids even though you would rather relax and do nothing. Putting the needs of others ahead of your own is never easy. It takes strength, willpower, and discipline, Annie."

Anne was at a loss for a reply at first, and then she turned to her sisters who were once again staring dazedly at Will. "Oh, for heaven's sake snap out of it and stop simpering. And you." She stood and looked at Will. "Stop filling their heads with unrealistic daydreams." She stomped to the edge of the room and turned back to yell, "And stop calling me Annie."

The other occupants of the room watched her go and regarded Will with interest written on their faces.

"Can it really be like that, Will?" Libby asked. "Do some men take care of their women that way?"

He nodded, and after a thoughtful pause he spoke. "Who took care of your mother when she was sick?"

"We did," Maggie answered cheerfully. Will guessed she was too young for the memories to be painful. Not so for her older sisters. Kitty's eyes held a slight shadow, but Libby's expression was pinched and haunted. How much worse had it been for Anne, the oldest? He remembered her sobbing in his arms and his chest tightened. He waited until the younger girls vacated the kitchen before he asked Libby his next question.

"How did your father react to your mother's illness?"

Libby let out a pent up breath. "Not well. He threw himself into the ranch. It was almost like if he made the ranch really prosperous he could somehow save Mom, and then when it didn't work, he lost interest in everything. Anne had to take over the ranch when she was twelve, at least for a while until Dad came back into focus. He wasn't comfortable with any signs of her illness, either. They made him crazy. When she lost her hair, he destroyed the tack room in the barn."

"And how did your mother react?" He picked up the dish towel to dry, and she noted the action with surprise.

"Let me guess, real men don't dry dishes," he said dryly.

"Some people believe that, not me," she said. "Anyway, Mom was unbothered by Dad. She understood him. She loved him. She had a way of reaching him that none of the rest of us can. He was softer with her and with us when she was alive. He and Anne are two peas in a pod. Neither is good with feelings. It seems to be the way of life now that Mom is gone. Everyone thinks I'm a softhearted simpleton for crying. The girls are okay because they're young and everyone expects them to be soft, but I worry for them. I don't want them to become closed off and hard like..." Her words died off, but they both knew what she was thinking.

Like Anne.

CHAPTER 4

*A*nne clenched her fists and leaned against the wall outside the kitchen. So that was how people saw her: A rock solid, heartless shell of a woman. They had no idea what she really felt, or how deeply. Emotions were a luxury she couldn't afford. She had a ranch to run, and sisters to raise, and a father to take care of. She had a duty to do, and there was no one else to do it. Resentment and sadness couldn't be in her vocabulary because if she allowed them to gain a foothold, they would overwhelm her. She would sink under the weight of them, and she would never be free of them again. No. It was better to feel nothing, to steel her spine and press on as if she hadn't a care in the world.

She squeezed her eyes tighter and pounded her clenched fist on her thigh. It was all his fault; he, with his probing questions, stirred everything up and made her think about things she shouldn't. His kind gentle eyes appeared in her mind and she stifled a groan. He looked at her as if he wanted to help her. *Her.* She didn't need him; she didn't need anybody. The sooner he left, the better.

The problem, she realized the next day, was her sisters. They looked at the newcomer as if he were decked out in silver armor and sitting atop a white stallion. She expected as much from Libby and

Maggie, they wore their hearts on their sleeves, but Kitty had always been the dependable, rational one. Why was she turning traitor?

It didn't take Anne long to figure out why. As if he had some sixth sense about how to appeal to them he used a different tactic on each sister. He insisted on tutoring Maggie and Kitty, since that was the reason he was here, and Anne stood in the doorway to observe. It was almost like he was two different people.

With Kitty he was scholarly, like a college professor. He talked up to her, and not down. He challenged her to listen and understand what he was saying without dumbing anything down. Kitty blossomed under his approach. She looked for ways to exceed his expectations, and found them. Instead of praising her, he rewarded her by giving her advanced essays far beyond her years. His trust in her abilities was more important to her than any words of adulation. Anne couldn't remember the last time she saw her quiet little sister so excited.

Maggie, on the other hand, had little interest in schoolwork. She expected to be bored, but Will anticipated her. He related all of her lessons to the outdoors. He found a story about lost Indian treasure in Montana, and had her measuring out and calculating distances on a map so she didn't realize she was doing math.

At night he told them stories and asked them questions about themselves and the ranch. Libby, Kitty, and Maggie so badly wanted to put their faith in him and accept him completely, but they sensed Anne's reticence, and held back on her account.

She was conflicted, too. She was torn between her desire to stick close to the house in order to keep an eye on him and her desire to flee to the wide open spaces to forget all about him. Every minute of his presence chipped away at her hard-earned defenses, and the impending vulnerability made her irritable. Who was this man that he should affect her so? What right did he have to come here and question the status quo?

And question it he did. He asked pointed questions so surreptitiously that not even the usually skeptical Kitty knew what he was doing, but Anne did because almost every question was about her in some way. Why was she the foreman? How long had she been the foreman? Did the men really defer to her as their leader? Could she really do all the work a man did? The questions made her want to prove her abilities to him and at the same time question why she should have to. Why *was* she the foreman? Why *did* she do the things she did?

By the morning of the third day she'd had enough. She was convinced he meant her sisters no harm, so she decided to leave him and spend the day riding fences.

But to her consternation when she arrived at the barn at first light he was there waiting for her.

"Running away?" he asked, and his infuriating half-smile made her want to punch him. He acted as if he knew her, but of course he didn't. He only thought he did.

"No," she answered crisply. "I have work to do." She saddled her horse in silence, hoping he would take the hint and leave, but he didn't.

"I thought I would come with you today so you wouldn't have to worry about me being alone with your sisters all day. Unless you've decided you trust me now."

She jerked her horse's cinch. He had her in a quandary, and he knew it. If she told him to stay at the house it was tantamount to an admission of her trust in him. There was no way she was doing that. But if she didn't, it meant he would be riding with her all day. Suddenly the possibilities in the situation occurred to her, and she smiled. He probably didn't have much experience with horses. Some were more spirited than others. This could be an interesting opportunity to show him what ranch life was really all about.

"Sure, you can ride with me." She turned to face him and her smile died. He was holding the reins to Maggie's pony, and *he* was smiling as if he had guessed her thoughts.

"Maggie thought her pony might be the safest choice for me today," he said. "She was concerned I might ride one of the more unmanageable horses and then want to leave if I fell off."

Anne pressed her lips together in a grim line. "Fine." She mounted her horse in a practiced, fluid motion, and waited while he mounted his with less effort than she would have guessed.

"I have long legs," he explained as if he could hear her thoughts. His ability to guess what she was thinking was disconcerting. She considered herself to be an island and he was making her feel like a peninsula, too connected.

"What are we working on today?" he asked.

"*I* am riding fences," she said.

"What does that mean?"

"It means I'm riding along the fencerows checking for anything that needs repaired. With so many acres of cattle a fence break could cost a huge amount of money in cattle loss, so we have to stay on top of maintenance."

"You're very knowledgeable," he commented.

"I should be. It's been my life since my birth."

She had no idea she sounded sad when she said that, he thought. "What kind of music do you like?"

The abrupt subject change caught her off guard. "Opera." She said it before she had time to think, but he seemed unsurprised.

"Is there much opera music in the middle of Montana?" he asked.

"There's country music, and that's pretty much it, but we do have satellite, and the Internet."

"How did you become interested in opera?"

"My mom," she said softly in the gentle tone she reserved for speaking of her mother. "She was cultured and well-educated, and she wished the same for us." Her face closed up and her features turned hard. That dream was over now. College for her was as likely as a trip to the moon.

"Does that have something to do with why I'm here?" Will asked.

Anne sighed. She wasn't used to talking so much. "I suppose. As you found out town is an hour away. That's where the nearest schools are. When my mother was alive she was adamant we attend. She wanted us to receive a proper education and be socialized with other kids." She paused, remembering. "She used to drive us to and from school every day. Two hours because it was important to her. Then, after, it wasn't practical anymore. There was no one to drive us, and Libby and I couldn't be spared from our duties. So we dropped out and started to do home school. But because we've been doing it on our own, our education is lacking, especially Maggie and Kitty. So Dad had the idea of sending for a tutor." Her tone let him know what she thought of the idea.

They rode in silence for a while. Will was feeling the saddle in places he didn't know existed, but Anne didn't seem bothered by the journey. He would die before he would admit his discomfort, though. She already saw him as slightly more than a girl. He had no intention of adding to that misconception. Finally, when he was so stiff and sore he was sure he would never walk upright again she reined her horse to a stop and dismounted.

She checked a fence that looked perfectly fine to him, but she frowned as she tested it and pulled a hammer and nails out of her saddlebag. She pounded a few nails, tested again, and then seemed satisfied.

"Need any help?" he asked.

She spared him a brief, dismissive glance, but otherwise didn't respond.

"Time for lunch?" he tried again. He wanted to do anything to prolong the break. She checked the sky to gauge the time.

"Don't you believe in these?" He tapped his watch.

"Machines malfunction. The sun doesn't," she replied.

He smiled and withdrew the lunch Libby packed for him. "Libby packed enough for both of us, I think."

Anne leaned close to him and looked in the bag. "No, that's a normal amount. She's used to making food for people who work up an appetite."

"By your subtle inference, I take it to mean I do nothing to burn calories," he said.

"I'm sure using your brain is exhausting," she said.

"It really is." He set out the food Libby had prepared, amazed any one person could consume it all. Surely Anne was exaggerating. He studied her as she ate in silence. Her white Stetson hat was perched jauntily on her head but, unlike the first time they met, her hair wasn't tucked under her hat. Today it spilled out in long waves around her shoulders. Her face was small and heart shaped, and her already large brown eyes looked larger in her elfin face. She ate delicately, although she ate a lot. When she became aware of his inspection, she tipped her hat down so it hid her face from view. She was intriguing, and alluring, and he had never met anyone like her. She was utterly interesting to him, and he found her mix of vulnerability and steel captivating.

She felt, rather than saw, his continued inspection. She tipped her hat so low it toppled off her head. Reflexively he lunged for it. He caught it, but the action brought him close to her face and they froze. Her lips parted, and her head tipped up slightly. His face descended toward hers, but before their lips met he found himself sprawled flat on his back and staring up at the sky.

"Around here we don't take kisses without permission," Anne said. She sat on her knees and towered over him with her hands folded over her chest.

"Where I'm from we don't assume someone is about to kiss us," he said, although he had been about to kiss her. Her constant attempts to lance his pride were starting to have their desired effect.

She started to stand, but he grabbed her ankle to hold her back. And then he realized he shouldn't have when she immediately flew into a frenzy. At first he was simply trying to avoid being injured by her flying feet and fists, but then his own temper was stirred, and it turned into an all out wrestling match. Will wasn't sure how she accomplished it, but she seemed to be all arms and legs everywhere at once. She didn't fight like other girls he had seen. There was no screaming, crying, hair pulling or biting. There was only a quiet determination to beat him, and what was most disconcerting to Will was how close she came to doing it. Eventually, though, he triumphed and pinned her arms behind her back.

"It might interest you to know I box with a trainer for fun," he said.

If Anne was surprised she didn't show it. "And you think working out in a gym is equal to doing real work."

"Maybe not, but being a man makes me bigger and stronger than you. There aren't many women who can take down a man, especially a man who is almost a foot taller than them." He said it conversationally, and as he spoke he relaxed his grip on her, which he soon realized was another mistake. His temper had fled, but hers hadn't. As soon as she was free, she pounced on him again knocking him to the ground.

Will almost felt sorry for her. She was struggling hard to prove to him she was strong, but it wasn't working. Why was she fighting so hard? What did she have to gain by beating him? They tangled together for an unknown length of time until they were both breathless, sweaty, and exhausted, and then one of her cowboy boots clipped his jaw and his soft feelings fled. It was time to end this ridiculousness. With a renewed surge of strength he captured her and pinned her fully beneath him.

Her long hair was in a snarl, and she was covered in dust and breathing hard, but he found her adorable. He smiled as he took in her appearance, but his smile fled when he saw her eyes. She was afraid. Of him. And no wonder, he thought with a flash of shame. She was tiny, and he was holding her down with all his weight. He was a stranger to her and they were in the middle of nowhere. Of course she would be afraid of him, what girl in her right mind wouldn't be? He couldn't believe he had allowed her to get to him so completely he had lost all sense and acted in this manner. His mother would never forgive him for acting so inappropriately. He immediately released her and rolled onto his back in a submissive position.

"I'm sorry, Annie," he said contritely. "I should never have done that. I would never, ever do anything to hurt you."

She continued to lie quietly on her back and they remained side by side for a few minutes. He wondered what she was thinking. He was feeling guilt, remorse, and something like regret that it was over. Despite the fact that he knew it was wrong to wrestle with a girl, it had been fun. He had enjoyed the opportunity to hold her, even though it had been like holding a live catfish.

"Too bad you're leaving, Ashley, because I would enjoy the opportunity to beat you."

"What are you talking about? I beat you twice."

"Doesn't mean you would a third time," she said. She sat up and dusted herself off. "I don't like losing, and it's not something I do often. All I need to do is revise my strategy, and I'm sure I can take you." She said it conversationally, as if they were talking about the weather instead of a wrestling match.

He smiled up at her. "Is this something you do often? Is this how you get your men to listen to you? Do you threaten to beat them up if they don't do what they're told?"

She didn't crack a smile. "They do what they're told because they know I'm right. Always. They listen to me because I've proved myself over and over, and more than physically. I can brand and pull calves as well as, or better than, any of them, and they know it. Just because you think I'm weak and helpless doesn't mean they do."

"You? Weak and helpless? Are you kidding me? That was the best workout I ever had. I feel like I should pay you what I pay my trainer. If you ever decide to give up ranching, you have a career in martial arts." He stood and dusted himself off, but not before he caught a hint of a smile on her lips.

CHAPTER 5

"Who's your story Ashley?" Anne asked as they started to ride fences once more. "You're ever curious about us, but you haven't told us anything about you."

"That's because I'm boring," Will said. "I live in Pittsburgh and have a double major in business and history. I'm the youngest of three boys, and my childhood is full of the usual trauma they inflicted on me. My mom and I are close, my dad not so much, and that's about it."

"And what's your favorite music?" Anne asked.

He smiled. "Everything. I have a tin ear and can't carry a tune, so I'm in awe of anyone who can. I like jazz, hip hop, country, reggae, swing. Oh, and opera." He winked at her, and she didn't react.

"Does that type of flirting work on other girls?"

"Yes, and usually very well. I've had lots and lots of girlfriends." He paused to gauge her reaction. "Jealous?"

"Incredulous."

"What about you?"

"I've never had a girlfriend," she said.

"If I didn't know better I would think the cowgirl was displaying a sense of humor."

"This robot has feelings," she said defensively.

"I never for a minute thought you didn't have feelings," he said. "I've been at the receiving end of too much of your anger to doubt it. Anger is usually an indicator of a passionate nature. Are you passionate, Annie? If you're not sure I could help you find out."

"Do you know your way to the train station, Ashley? If you're not sure I could help you find out."

He laughed again. "Annie, you're a delight."

She stuck her tongue out at him and urged her horse forward.

He smiled at the back of her head. Maybe that was why he was so fascinated by her. With other girls it was so easy. He wasn't drop dead gorgeous, but he was nice enough looking, and girls seemed to find him attractive. More than that, though, he knew how to talk to them. He knew what they needed and was happy to provide it. Girls liked him; it was a fact of his life. Anne, though, was something altogether different. She almost seemed to loathe him, and it would be a challenge to try and change her mind.

"What's your favorite opera?" he asked when he caught up with her.

"*Lakme.*" She said it warily. She wasn't yet sure she could trust him with the information.

"What is it about?"

"It's about a British soldier who falls in love with an Indian girl. Of course their love is forbidden, and her mother tries to kill him, but she nurses him back to health in the forest. Then one of his friends convinces him of his duty to his country, and so he lets her go."

"What happens to her?" he asked.

"She kills herself."

"Why do you like it so much?"

"The officer puts duty above his selfish desires."

He studied her profile as he thought that over. Is that what she did? Was there a chance she didn't enjoy ranching? Maybe she liked ranching but didn't enjoy watching out for her siblings. No, that wasn't so. She seemed to delight in her younger sisters, and Libby had the brunt of their care, anyway. Most likely she was talking about the ranch, if she was talking about herself at all. Maybe she wasn't. Maybe she was blissfully happy and enjoyed sad opera for no other reason other than the beautiful music.

"I would like to hear it," he said.

She looked at him to gauge his sincerity. "You can borrow the CD before you leave."

She spoke of his leaving as a bygone conclusion, and if her father was anything like her she was probably right. He would probably take one look at Will and make him leave without giving him the chance to plead his case. But the more time he spent at the ranch the more he wanted to stay there. He couldn't leave yet. He wanted to help Kitty and Maggie; he had already helped them learn a few new things in the two days he had been working with them, and the feeling was addictive. Given the entire summer they could grow by leaps and bounds academically. He also enjoyed learning about the ranch. He liked asking Libby questions and eating her delicious food while she answered. More than any of that, though, there was Anne. If he left her now without unraveling the mystery that surrounded her, he was sure he would always regret it. For the rest of the journey he tried to think of a way to stay, but by the time they returned to the house he still hadn't found it.

Anne was suspicious of his new silence. She was annoyed by his chattiness, but, now that he was quiet, she wished he would talk. His calmness unnerved her. And she had to admit she was flattered by his attention and flirtation. He was a blip in her otherwise dreary existence. She could tell he was the type girls liked. Her sisters certainly did. That he should select her as the object of his desire, however briefly, was nice. Maybe she had been too hard on him. After all, it was his first time on a ranch. He couldn't be expected to act like the cowboys she had known forever. By the time they reached the barn she had convinced herself she was being unfair and his new stillness was due to her coolness.

"Ashley," she said. "I hope you'll have fun here for the remainder of your stay." She dismounted her horse and began grooming it.

Will dismounted his horse and looked at the back of her head while she worked on her horse. Maybe he would have to leave here. If so, he wanted to have one good memory of her to take with him. He came to stand close behind her and caught the unique scent of her. It was a combination of leather and something floral, and he smiled. How apropos that her smell should be something feminine masked by leather.

"Annie," he said softly. He rested his hand on hers to still it, and she turned to look at him. They stood staring at each other. For once her big eyes were soft when they looked at him and not full of suspicion or anger. He wanted to kiss her, but he was afraid of scaring her off. "Spend the evening with me. It could be my last night here. I want to remember you."

"I don't think I should," she said slowly, and without much conviction.

"Please," he said. He took her free hand and kissed her fingertips. She watched him do it and swallowed hard.

"All right," she agreed in a near whisper. As if they were working against her will, her fingertips caressed his lips and moved to trace the outline of his face. He closed his eyes and allowed her fingers to have free reign over his features. When she was finished, he opened his eyes and the spell was broken.

"I have work to do," she said in her usual rough tone.

"Can I help you?" he offered.

"No. Thank you," she added brusquely. She turned her back to him and resumed grooming her horse.

He walked to the edge of the barn and paused. "You'll still go out with me tonight?"

She stopped and froze with her hand on the curry comb. "Yes." She said it only loudly enough for him to hear.

He turned and headed toward the house. He wasn't sure when he had ever felt so happy, and he whistled as he walked.

As soon as he left, Anne set down the comb and allowed her shaking knees to collapse onto the soft hay. What happened here? How did he get her to agree to spend the evening with him? Of course she couldn't. She would have to make up an excuse to get out of it.

She felt unsettled, not only because she had gotten herself into this mess but because she didn't want to get out of it. He was strange and different, but he was temporary. Shouldn't she be allowed to have this one brief moment of time to know what it felt like to be a normal girl?

She rested her head in her hands. No, of course she couldn't. She was a horrible person for even thinking it. Was her head turned by the first handsome boy who paid her any attention? Apparently so, if her strong desire to be with Will tonight was any indication. They would most likely go walking in the moonlight. She knew all the deserted areas of the ranch. She would take him to one that was especially beautiful, and he would kiss her.

Her heartbeat quickened. What would it be like to kiss Will? She had only ever kissed one boy, and thoughts of kissing someone else made her feel both excited and afraid. Whatever happened, she could not allow him to kiss her. It would be disastrous, and she wouldn't allow it. The thought that it had already almost happened once today came up to assault her, and she groaned. What was wrong with her? Wasn't she the one who was always chastising Maggie and Libby for having their heads in the clouds? Yet here she sat daydreaming of a handsome stranger who could very well wreck her life. Her horse whinnied and pranced to remind her she wasn't done being groomed.

"Sorry," Anne said contritely. She finished grooming her horse and pushed all other thoughts from her mind. She would deal with tonight when the moment came, and she would do the right thing, no matter what.

CHAPTER 6

If Will was feeling any nerves about their approaching evening together, he didn't show them during supper. He was his usual charming and gregarious self and had her sisters eating out of the palm of his hand. Anne had half a mind to reprimand them for being so easily swayed by a handsome face. Then she remembered her promise to go walking with him later, and her words died on her lips. Some example she was. Yet try as she might, she couldn't bring herself to cancel. He would be leaving tomorrow when her father returned, and she wanted to have this one last night to remember him by. But walking would be all they would do together. She wouldn't kiss him. She had to tell herself over and over because every time she pictured it, her resolve swayed.

The other girls noticed Anne's silence, but chalked it up to her continued distrust and dislike of Will. They felt bad about the way things were between the two, and worked even harder than normal to make Will feel welcome and liked.

As for Will, his thoughts centered on one thing: kissing Anne tonight in the moonlight. For the past few hours it had become his obsession and he could hardly wait until supper was over and he could have her to himself. She would melt into his embrace like she had in the car when she cried, and he would have the satisfaction of knowing he had brought out the utterly feminine side he knew she had buried deep inside her.

Libby stood to serve dessert when the clatter of hooves sounded in the yard. Kitty and Maggie looked at each other with smiles, but Anne sat up and froze in alarm. A few minutes later the front door banged shut and then the sound of heavy boot steps echoed throughout the house. Finally a young cowboy stood in the doorway and seemed to fill up the space there.

"I'm home, Chapman girls. Did you miss me?" he asked cheerfully, and gave them all a smile.

Libby stopped her preparations and whirled to face the newcomer with her hands on her hips. "Dobbie, did you purposely wallow in mud on your way home? Look at your boots."

The newcomer glanced down. "They're hardly dirty at all, Libby."

"So you admit they're a little dirty," she said.

"Some," he agreed.

"And yet you didn't pause to take them off before you trekked across my clean floors," she said, and two spots of color flushed her cheeks. Will was fascinated by the display. In the three days he had known Libby she hadn't once raised her voice or said an angry word. She seemed to be as sweet and gentle as Anne was prickly, but the sight of this dusty cowboy had wiped away any traces of her sweet nature.

"Oh, come on, Libby. I broke speed records to get back here to see you all. I beat your dad home by a full day. Doesn't that count for something?" He gave her a hopeful smile and eyed the dessert behind her.

"More dirt on your boots, apparently," she said. "You get out of this kitchen and take off those shoes before I come take them off for you."

He folded his arms over his chest. "Try and make me, little bit."

She grabbed the nearest item, which happened to be a skillet. "This is your last warning. Take off your boots."

He pressed his lips into a thin line and slowly shook his head.

She grasped the pan more tightly, and, when he saw she was serious, he turned and ran from the room.

"I'm going to go lie on your bed and stomp my feet," he called over his shoulder.

"So help me, Dobbie, if I find one trace of dirt in my bed, you will never eat my pie again," Libby yelled, and they were both gone.

Will watched the scene with an amused smile. Maggie and Kitty looked unaffected, as if it were an everyday occurrence. He couldn't tell what expression Anne wore because she was staring at her plate with sudden intensity.

"Was that her boyfriend?" Will asked. He wondered why Libby hadn't mentioned him when he asked about eligible people to date.

"No, that's Anne's boyfriend," Maggie said. "Dobbie. They've been dating forever. They're going to get married."

"Maggie," Anne snapped. "We're not engaged." She stood abruptly so her chair scraped roughly on the floor, and then stalked from the room without another word or glance.

Will tried to listen to Maggie's happy chatter as if his world hadn't imploded. Anne had a boyfriend? A serious boyfriend she planned to one day marry? Who was the mysterious cowboy? No one bothered to explain it to him, and Kitty and Maggie were too little to involve in his schemes and plots surrounding Anne. He would have to wait until Libby returned and ask her.

Thankfully she returned a short time later. She set the skillet gently on the counter and smoothed a hand over her already immaculate hair. For someone who had taken flight through the house she appeared unruffled. Her dress and hair were perfectly in place, as they always were whenever Will saw her.

"Who was that?" He wasted no time in asking.

Maggie and Kitty had left by now, and Libby turned to him with a knowing smile. "Aren't you a curious cat, Will? So many questions, but all of them have a central theme."

He gave her a sheepish smile. A camaraderie had developed between them over the past few days. Whatever fleeting interest she had in him had quickly disappeared. She felt like a sister to him, and he knew she felt the same sort of comfortable affection for him. They were kindred spirits and nothing more.

"To answer your question, that is Dobbie. He's second in command after Anne, and he's also her boyfriend."

"What's their story? How did they meet?" Will asked. He pushed his dessert away. He suddenly had no appetite.

Libby talked while she cleaned the kitchen. "They met at birth, I think. They're the same age and he was our nearest neighbor to the west until he was fourteen, and then he moved in with us."

"Why?" Will asked. His tone was gentle because he sensed there was some sad reason for the move.

Libby looked around to make sure they were alone. "His parents were killed in a house fire. There was no one else to take him. He was close to our family already, and Dad had always wanted a son. He lived in the house for a year and then moved to the bunkhouse when the last foreman left. He has his own room and bathroom there, like a private apartment. He's a part of our family, and as I'm sure my sisters told you, he's Anne's boyfriend. They've been matched since birth, and it's an established fact they'll marry one day." She attacked the pot in her hand with intensity and scowled as she scrubbed a particularly stubborn spot.

Will studied her as she scrubbed the pot. He had some thoughts on the Dobbie situation, but it wasn't the time or place to voice them. "What's your favorite music, Libby?"

"Will, you're an interesting boy, you know that? But I don't want to tell you my favorite music. You'll make fun of me."

"You really think so?" he asked.

"I guess not. I love show tunes, you know, like from musicals. I think the world would be a happier place if everybody sang what they felt all the time."

He smiled. "I like show tunes, too, and I happen to agree with you. Maybe I would sing my feelings if I could sing. Instead I wear them on my sleeve."

"Join the club."

"Is it safe to come in?" a voice asked from the doorway and Will turned to see Dobbie peeking around the corner.

Libby turned to look, too. "Let me see your feet," she commanded.

He stepped inside. He was wearing boots, but they weren't the same ones as before and they were clean.

"Come in," she said, and then set aside the pot she was scrubbing and opened the oven door. She took out a heaping plate and set it in front of Dobbie. He looked at the plate with something like reverence.

"Thanks, Lib."

She patted his head and turned back to her dishes.

After a few minutes of silence while Dobbie attacked his meal with a vengeance he finally wiped his hand on his napkin and held it out to Will.

"I'm Dobbie. Maggie told me there was some sort of mix up, and you're the new tutor." His tone was friendly, but his eyes were piercing, protective, and fierce. He was judging Will and weighing his character.

"I'm Will Ashley," Will said.

Dobbie nodded and returned his attention to his food.

"The girls have been filling me in on the ranching way of life," Will said. "I know nothing about it. I'm from the city. What do you do here?"

"Whatever Anne tells me to," Dobbie said, and he and Libby laughed.

Will found Dobbie as intriguing as Anne, although not in quite the same way. He had no desire to kiss Dobbie, thank goodness, but he was obviously a manly sort of man, the sort of man Anne was used to. Why didn't it bother him to take direction from a girl? Was it because he loved her so much? Despite Will's sensitive nature he would never allow a girl to direct his every move. Was there a power struggle between them, or was Dobbie biding his time until the marriage? Or was there a less sinister option? Was Anne really so good at her job the men naturally deferred to her as their leader? He thought it was unusual that as time went on he found more questions than answers in this place, but it made him all the more desperate to stay. It would be worth it to satisfy his raging curiosity.

Libby seemed to have a sixth sense about when Dobbie wanted a refill and kept his plate and glass filled without his asking. Dobbie always said, "Thanks, Lib," in a distracted sort of way, but when her back was turned, he watched her work. Will decided to try an experiment.

"I've been trying to get to know the girls the last few days," he told Dobbie. "I was wondering if you know Anne's favorite type of music."

"Sure," Dobbie said easily. "It's country."

"And Libby? What's her favorite music?" Will asked, and held his breath while he waited for the answer.

Dobbie rolled his eyes. "Show tunes, if you can believe it. Figures it would be something frilly and brainless." He ducked when Libby threw a wet dishrag at him. "Woman, don't push me," he said, and stood to toss the rag back in the sink. "I think I'll have my dessert in my room because I'm about dead on my feet and tomorrow's a long day of catching up." He turned to Will. "Nice to meet you, Mr. Ashley. I hope you enjoyed your stay. Let me know if there's anything further you need." He gave Will one more studying look, and then picked up a plate of pie and exited the kitchen.

Will waited until the door closed behind him and then he also exited the house. He studied the horizon as the sun was setting on the ranch and inhaled air so pure it almost hurt to breathe. There was no pollution here, unless you counted the smell of horse and cow manure, but somehow even that pungent, earthy scent smelled good. There was a lone mountain in the distance, one of a few strays that denoted the beginning of the Rocky Mountains. He knew there were wolves, grizzlies, elk, and moose somewhere out there but you would never know it from the peaceful serenity of the house and barns. The only sounds were the lowing of the cows and the neighing of the horses.

Some instinct told him Anne was in the barn. Most likely she wanted to be alone, but he went to her anyway. She was like a drug to him, and he couldn't stay away. At first he didn't see her, and then he caught sight of her legs dangling over the edge of the hay loft. She tried to draw up her knees and disappear, but it was too late. He ascended the ladder and sat beside her in the soft hay.

"Hiding?" he asked.

"No," she said. Her voice was thick with repressed emotion.

"Were you crying?" he asked.

"No, I never cry." He gave her a look. "Almost never. I hadn't cried in a long time."

"That doesn't seem healthy," he said.

"Healthy is doing your duty without complaint. Tears are a wasteful luxury." She picked up a piece of hay and began to dismantle it into tiny shards.

"Tears are a release of great emotion and not always negative emotion. Sometimes people cry when they're happy."

She almost smiled at that. "Libby does. She cries over everything."

"You don't sound like you think less of her because of it," he commented.

"She's Libby. People make allowances for her because she's soft and sweet and girly."

"Don't people make allowances for you for the same reason?"

"I don't need allowances," she said.

He wasn't so sure about that, but he didn't feel like arguing. "How long have you and Dobbie been together?"

Her brow furrowed as she tried to calculate the time. "I don't ever remember not being together. We've always been friends and neighbors, and so we spent a lot of time together. A dating relationship was expected, and it developed naturally. I guess when we were about fourteen, so we've been together four years."

He whistled. "That's a long time. If you're getting married someday you must love him a lot."

"He's my best friend, besides Libby."

Will nodded. "Friendship is important in a marriage, I guess. I suppose you have romantic feelings for him, too." He peeked at her out of the corner of his eye.

"I," she started, and then paused. "I suppose so." She had always thought so. She thought the gentle affection she felt for Dobbie was what passed for romance for other people. They had everything in common and they were a lot alike. Wasn't that love? If not, what was?

"Have you ever been in love?" she asked.

"I don't think so."

"How do you know when it's really love?"

"I think maybe you know, beyond all certainty," he said. "That's what my mom tells me, that when she looked at my dad she knew."

Anne nodded. "I don't remember my mom ever telling me anything like that about my dad, but I guess she loved him very much to leave her world and join his. Her father was a diplomat. They lived in New York City whenever they weren't in Belgium. She met my dad on vacation when she was my age. They stayed in touch and dated while she was in college. One day he showed up at her school and told her she was going to marry him, and so she did."

She was the most relaxed he had ever seen her, and he didn't want the magic to end. "Were her parents upset?"

"I imagine so, but they died in a plane crash soon after the wedding. I have an aunt who still lives in New York, but I barely know her. She sends cards and she came to visit once when Mom was sick." She sounded almost wistful when she spoke of the aunt and he wondered why. Was it because she yearned for family, or because she yearned for the excitement and adventure of the city? He lay back in the hay as she talked, and she followed suit. They lay a foot apart, not touching, but cocooned in the intimate silence of the barn.

"Tell me about your mom," he said. He stretched out his arm and rested his head on it.

"She was beautiful. She had brown hair, like me and all my sisters, and her eyes were brown, too. More than that, though, she was vivacious. She could and did do everything. She was talented in the kitchen like Libby, but she liked to do outdoor work like me and Maggie. And she was smart like Kitty. She never watched television, she read voraciously. She could make Dad laugh. She could make us all laugh, but she also had a temper, and she was a stickler for discipline and proper manners. She was the best and most wonderful part of my world, and when she died a part of me went with her." She paused and studied the stub of hay in her hand.

Will reached out and took her hand. She swallowed hard and clenched her jaw. "Cry," he commanded.

She shook her head.

He moved closer, grasped her shoulders and shook them slightly. "Cry, Annie."

She looked up at him with blazing anger and opened her mouth to protest, but a sob came out instead. Will pulled her close. She buried her face in his chest and wept, and it was a continuation of the day he first met her. He thought maybe she hadn't cried since the day her mother died and she had been storing up her tears, waiting for a release. Now that she had one she didn't seem to be able to stop. She sobbed for the better part of two hours, and when she was finished he didn't let her go. He kept one arm around her, and she clutched his shirt in her hand.

"I don't think I'll forget you," she said.

He smiled and smoothed his hand over her hair. He was certain he wouldn't forget her. Every girl would seem bland in comparison now. He wanted to ask her for a kiss, one kiss to treasure forever, but it wouldn't be fair. When he left she would return to her life and her boyfriend, and she would forever have the knowledge she had cheated on him. Instead he asked her to describe to him her favorite thing about ranch life, and then listened for another hour as she talked lovingly about riding horses on the open plain.

The next morning at breakfast was a sad affair. The Chapman sisters and Will all sensed his departure was imminent. Anne was resigned, but Libby, Maggie, and even Kitty had to fight hard to keep their tears at bay. Dobbie entered smiling cheerfully and then picked up on the mood at the table and lost his smile. He leaned down to give Anne a kiss on the cheek before sitting beside Maggie.

Will studied the couple as he ate his breakfast. There were no intimate looks or touches between them. After the perfunctory cheek kiss they talked about the ranch and the cattle drive he had been on, but they talked about it like business associates. Neither said they missed each other or made any loving reference whatsoever. Will sulked into his orange juice. He wished he could have broached the subject with Anne last night, but it was none of his business. If she wanted to marry this cowboy and be stuck in a passionless marriage, then so be it. It was her life, after all, and Dobbie seemed nice enough. Still, if by some miracle he stayed for the summer he would make it his mission to open her eyes to the truth in the situation. Dobbie didn't love Anne. He loved Libby, and Libby loved him. But all three characters in the sad little play were oblivious to their own feelings. Anne and Dobbie were soldiering on out of duty, or maybe out of habit, but some day one of them was going to get terribly hurt. Most likely it would be Libby. Dobbie and Anne would no doubt go through with their loveless union, and poor sweet Libby would be left to watch her sister married to the man she loved. Maybe she would go away, or maybe she would stay and become bitter.

Or maybe Will was wrong. Maybe his fanciful thoughts were born out of a desire to have Anne for his own. Maybe she and Dobbie loved each other very much, but neither was comfortable expressing it. Maybe the chemistry he sensed between Libby and Dobbie was genuine irritation with each other. He would probably never know. It would be one more mystery about his time here that would haunt him. This colorful cast of characters was now firmly etched in his brain, and he would be left forever wondering what became of them.

After breakfast Anne and Dobbie left to go to work, and Will insisted on tutoring Kitty and Maggie one last time. They became so immersed in their studies they forgot today was the last day, and they were all laughing uproariously when the front door slammed announcing their father's presence.

He walked into the living room weary from his day in the saddle, but then he stopped short at the sight of Will and gave him an appraising look. He was tall and well built with solid muscles that looked like they had been honed from tree trunks. His face was tan, and his hair was dark with liberal streaks of gray. His eyes were a dark shade of green. Will's mother would probably describe him as "distinguished."

"Who are you?" he asked with no preamble.

Will stood and held out his hand. "I'm Will Ashley, the tutor you hired."

Matt Chapman shook his hand, but didn't speak. Instead he stared at Will with an intensity that would have made a less confident man squirm. "I hired a woman."

Maggie did squirm. She looked at Will in panicked supplication. "No, sir, I'm very sorry to tell you there was a mix up in our communication, and you hired me," Will said.

Matt blew out a long, frustrated breath. "And you've been here alone with my girls for three days?"

"Yes, sir, but Anne has been keeping a close eye on me. I'm fairly certain if I stepped out of line she would have killed me and buried me in a shallow grave by now."

That garnered a small smile from the older man. "That's probably so." He looked at the books spread on the table between Kitty and Maggie. "You've actually been tutoring them?"

"Dad, we've learned so much," Kitty said enthusiastically. "Will is double majoring in business and history, but he's good at math, too. He's been teaching me some calculus. I never thought I would get the chance to study calculus so early."

"And he's been telling me about the French and Indian War," Maggie added. "I haven't been bored at all."

Libby appeared in the doorway.

"What's he been teaching you?" her father asked her. His look was suspicious as it darted from Libby to Will.

"She's been teaching me," Will volunteered. "My education on ranch life is sorely lacking, and Anne and Libby have been kind enough to fill me in."

"We've talked about literature, too," Libby added. "Will's a reader, like me."

Matt nodded, apparently satisfied with the tone of Libby's answer.

Just then Anne and Dobbie entered. Anne came into the room to stand by Will, but Dobbie remained standing in the doorway of the kitchen beside Libby.

"And what's your opinion of our tutor, little girl?" Matt asked Anne.

Anne shrugged.

Apparently that was something like praise because Matt looked at Will again with a new respect.

"We want him to stay," Kitty said. Anne gasped, but Kitty wouldn't look at her.

"We do, Daddy," Maggie added.

"Me, too," Libby added, ignoring Dobbie's frown.

Matt looked at Anne and waited for her to speak.

"He can't stay," Anne said.

"Why not?" Will asked; although, he already knew why. Anne had been afraid of him since he arrived. Last night's lowering of her guard was only because she thought he was leaving. "Don't you trust me?"

"I," she started and looked to Dobbie for help.

"He seems all right to me," Dobbie said, albeit reluctantly.

"But, but he can't," Anne said again. Her tone was desperate now.

"Is there some reason you're saying that?" Matt asked.

"He doesn't belong here," Anne said emphatically. "He's not cut out for ranch life."

"That's probably so," Matt agreed, "but he does seem cut out for tutoring. The girls like him, and it's too late to get someone else at this short notice." He turned to Will. "You can stay, but know I am keeping an eagle eye on you. And so help you if you take one step out of bounds, son." With that he turned and exited the house without waiting for a reply.

Dobbie wandered into the kitchen behind Libby, and Maggie and Kitty turned their eyes to their books. Only Anne and Will were left staring at each other.

Will smiled. "Looks like I'm staying, Annie."

Anne's mouth was still hanging open in shock, but she quickly closed it, her hands curling into fists. "Don't call me Annie," she said in a low threatening tone. "In fact, don't talk to me at all. Don't touch me. Don't come near me. Don't even look at me." She, too, turned on her heel and left the house the same way her father had gone.

Will smiled at the spot she vacated. It was going to be an interesting summer, indeed.

CHAPTER 8

For three weeks she avoided him completely, which wasn't difficult to do because Will was also busy. In addition to tutoring Maggie and Kitty, he had also started to help Libby prepare for her SAT exam. Because she was also busy the only way he was able to do it was to sit in the kitchen with her while she worked. Sometimes he helped her by drying dishes, snapping green beans, or ladling food into canning jars. Occasionally, Anne walked in and interrupted these sessions. She didn't comment, but her eyes were eloquent. She had strict definitions of what constituted men's work and women's work. Strange that she could cross over the line and do what was predominantly a man's job, but became uncomfortable when Will did "women's work."

During the day, Anne stayed away from the ranch doing whatever it was she did with her father and Dobbie. At night, she was exhausted from working all day and retired to her room soon after dinner. Will continued to observe Anne and Dobbie together, and what he saw made him sad. They got along well. They were a lot alike and had similar interests, and it was obvious they were friends. However, that's where the intimacy between them ended. If they touched, it was usually a perfunctory peck, and most of their conversations centered on the ranch. He continued to observe Dobbie and Libby together, as well. He had decided neither of them was aware of the tension broiling between them, and he asked Libby about it one day.

Dobbie entered the kitchen when Will was quizzing Libby on her vocabulary as she worked at the stove. As if she had a sixth sense about the young cowboy's presence she turned to the doorway and he froze. They both looked at his feet and the dirty boots he was wearing.

Libby looked outside. "It's not even raining. How did you manage to get so muddy?"

"It's not mud," he told her with a cocky grin. Then the smell hit them, and Will realized it was manure.

"You have so much gunk on those boots, I bet you can't even walk," Libby said.

"I can walk fine," Dobbie argued.

"Can you run?" Libby asked.

"Probably," he said, and his tone was wary.

Libby reached for her broom. "Then you'd better start because so help me, Dobbie, when I catch you you're going to get it." With that she took off toward him at a sprint and he ran off laughing like a naughty little boy.

"Did you catch him?" Will asked when she returned looking completely unruffled.

"I hit him five times before he took my broom and threatened to break it in two," Libby said casually, tucking her broom back in the closet.

"Do you love him?" Will asked.

"Sure I do. He drives me crazy, but he's family. Not officially, at least not until he and Anne get married."

He didn't read sadness in her tone, only acceptance of what everyone believed was a foregone conclusion. Will decided not to press the matter. If Libby wasn't aware of the sparks flying between her and her sister's boyfriend then he had no right to bring it up and add tension to an already tense situation. Upon observing Dobbie further he was convinced he had no idea of what was going on, either. He was a good and honest young man, and he would never date one sister while being in love with another if he realized that's what he was doing. Will also had to admit his reluctance to broach the subject was due to his own distrust in his motivation. If he pointed out the attraction simmering between Libby and Dobbie it might work to make Anne and Dobbie break up, but he didn't think it was fair to use his attraction to Anne to meddle in people's lives.

On the evenings Anne didn't go to bed early Will tried to steal a few minutes alone with her, but she outwitted him by always being with Dobbie, or her father, or one of her sisters. She wouldn't even meet his eyes over the supper table, and she never addressed conversation to him directly. Everyone noticed the tension and almost everyone chalked it up to Anne's usual taciturn nature. Everyone except her father.

"Why does my daughter avoid you like the plague?" Matt Chapman asked one night when he and Will happened to be alone on the porch.

As uncomfortable as it was Will knew he had to be truthful with his employer. "I like her, and she's scared of me because I make her feel things she hasn't wanted to feel in a long time. Things about your wife's passing."

Matt nodded. "Best to let sleeping dogs lie."

Will didn't want to argue, but he felt too strongly on the subject. "I'm not sure that's been working, at least for her. Girls feel things more deeply than we do, even girls like Anne who try to pretend they don't."

Matt thought that over. He may be a man's man, but he was fair and thoughtful. "You sound like my wife. She talked a lot about emotions. Never made much sense to me."

"You sound like my father. I don't make much sense to him, either."

Matt gave a small smile. "Well you've been doing a good job with the younger three. Maybe Anne needs some tutoring, too, but of a different kind. She's been different since her Mom died. Harder."

Will nodded. "I think the soft side of her is buried somewhere in there."

Matt shrugged, and Will guessed he had reached his limit of talking about feelings.

After his talk with Matt he was more determined than ever to break through Anne's reserve, but he couldn't gain a foothold. The separation was making him more fascinated with her, not less. He noticed everything about her, when she wore her hair up, and when she wore it down, the sweet way she watched her sisters, especially Maggie, as they talked over some event, the authoritative way she took charge whenever one of the ranch hands had a question. He was all together entranced and afraid he was turning into a lovesick puppy at the age of twenty. He didn't understand himself. He had never lacked for female attention before, and he had thought he was happy with the girls he dated, but Anne challenged those assumptions. What had he ever seen in other girls? No one had ever affected him like she did, and she was almost driving him to distraction. If not for the progress he was making with Maggie, Kitty, and Libby's studies he would have lost concentration completely.

Things probably would have gone on much the same if not for one pivotal event. One day after breakfast, but before lunch, Anne ran into the kitchen closer to panicking than Will had ever seen her.

"You have to help me," she said, and then took his hand and dragged him behind her without giving him the opportunity to question her or protest. She led him to the barn where a cow was lowing in obvious distress. Anne began setting out medieval looking instruments, all without a word on her part.

"Anne?" Will said it questioningly.

"We have to pull her calf," Anne said. "I know you're probably squeamish, but everyone else is out and I need help."

He scowled at her assumption he was helpless. "I'm not squeamish; I don't know what I'm doing."

"Hand me that lubricant, please," she said. The distress in her voice was obvious so he didn't plague her with unnecessary questions about the process. He only hoped she would tell him what she needed him to do instead of making him guess. He handed her a vat of lubricating jelly and watched, fascinated, while she poured it in the cow's birth canal.

"Calf jack," she said shortly. At first he thought she was calling him names, or giving some bizarre instruction, but then she held up the strange looking contraption and he guessed it was used to pull the calf out. She reached her hand into the birth canal again and fastened the implement around the calf's two front legs.

"I'm going to pull. All I need you to do is hold the tail out of the way. When the calf comes out tear off the placenta," she said. She got down on her knees and when the cow started to contract she started to pull. Immediate sweat broke out on her forehead and her face turned red with the effort. She was grunting and straining, but to no avail. The calf remained inside its mother.

"Let me pull," he said. She gave him a dubious look. "Annie, you may be strong, but you're still a girl. Move aside and let me do it." The calf must have been very important to her because she moved aside without further protest.

"You have to pull it out and down, one leg at a time until the head is out," she said. She ran a soothing hand over the cow's side, and talked calmly to her. Will felt the contraction and exerted more force than he ever had. Slowly, slowly the cow's head and feet started to emerge.

"Relax when she relaxes," Anne coaxed. "Stop pulling, but don't let the calf go back in." On the next pull the calf's head fully emerged. Anne tore the placenta away and cleared its nose. Will pulled and tugged until his arms shook with exertion. He didn't think he had ever used so much energy or strength in his entire life. Finally, when he felt like he was all used up the calf was completely delivered. It lay still and unbreathing on the hay. Ann took a twig of the hay and poked it in each nostril, whether to clear it or to try and agitate the calf he didn't know, but either way it worked. The calf started to stir and snort. Once the calf was fully viable, Anne released the chains from its legs, and then dragged it around to its mother.

She turned her back to Will and started to clean up, but Will sat still in the hay and watched her. He tried to think of all the girls he knew and picture them in Anne's place, delivering a calf and then calmly cleaning up. It was impossible. There was no one like her, and it was then he realized he was falling in love with her, or maybe he was already all the way there. Either way he was desperate to reclaim whatever connection they'd shared when he first arrived.

"Why were you so upset?" he asked. He guessed she had delivered hundreds of calves in her lifetime. He wondered why this one should worry her.

"This calf's parentage was expensive. The bull he came from cost a small fortune. We can't stand to lose any of his calves, and I could tell this was going to be a tough delivery. I already had to turn the calf before you arrived."

"You turned this calf around?" he asked, and all of the awe he felt showed in his voice.

"That's not so unusual."

"It is for me."

To his surprise she turned and smiled at him. "Welcome to the country, Ashley." She winked and returned to her duties.

He smiled at the back of her head. "You've been avoiding me."

She stiffened. Probably the euphoria from their successful delivery had made her lower her guard temporarily and now that it was wearing off she would come to her senses. "I have a boyfriend."

"And he doesn't allow you to be friends with anyone else?"

She gave him a dubious look. "Friends, really? Is that all you want from me?"

"No, but if that's all you're willing to give then that's what I'll take." She didn't answer, and he could sense her wavering. "Come on, Annie, don't be a chicken."

She threw something at his head that narrowly missed him. "I'm not a chicken, and don't call me Annie."

He stood. "You are a chicken. You've been hiding from me like a scared little girl, and I'll call you whatever I please."

She put her hands on her hips and faced him again. "Since when are you the king who issues edicts to me?"

"Since you've been avoiding me and making me crazy. And for the record, I'm not now, nor have I ever been, a fading flower. I may be able to talk comfortably about my emotions, but it doesn't make me weak, which you would know if you weren't too scared to get near me."

Her eyes flashed fire. "I'm not scared of you. I'm not scared of anything."

"Prove it," he said.

"I've been proving it all my life," she returned.

"Then there's no need to stop now. Spend time with me and stop running from me."

"You're a real pain, you know that, Ashley?"

He smiled because he knew he had won. "Believe it or not, you're not the first girl to tell me." She frowned, and his smile widened.

CHAPTER 9

*H*e spent the remainder of that day with her.

"Aren't you supposed to be tutoring my sisters?" she asked.

"I had already declared today to be a holiday. They're doing great, but they needed a day off. I was going to spend the day in the kitchen with Libby," he said.

"You spend a lot of time with Libby."

"Who else is there? You've been avoiding me."

"It never occurred to you to spend time by yourself?" she asked.

"No. I'm a social butterfly, and I'm needy," he said.

She tried to hide her smile, but couldn't. "I probably could have guessed that."

"No you couldn't. You seem to have some preconceived notion of me I would love to dispel."

"And how do you plan to do that? By talking me to death about your *feelings*." She shuddered.

"No, by getting you to talk about *your* feelings. I know they're in there; you can't pretend you don't have any."

She pressed her lips together and slammed a cupboard. "My feelings are none of your business."

"What if they're about me?" he asked.

"I don't have any feelings about you," she said.

"None? Not even loathing?"

She smiled again. "Well, maybe a little bit of loathing."

"Good. Dislike is a small leap from love. Indifference is the only thing that could discourage me."

"Are you always this irrepressible, Ashley?"

"No. You're bringing out the extremes in my temperament. So, what's next on your agenda, Madame Foreman?"

"I'm moving some cattle from the east to the west pasture today. Are you up for some time in the saddle?"

"Sure. I've almost recovered the full use of my legs from our last day in the saddle," he said.

"What do you do all day in Pittsburgh?" she asked.

He had to think about that. What did he do all day? "During the year I'm in school, so I go to classes."

"What do you do at night?" she asked.

"I go out. With friends or with a girl."

"And where do you go?" She sounded truly curious.

"To eat, or to dance, or to a movie." He paused. "Have you ever been to a movie?"

"A few times. There's a theater in Billings, but it's so far away that it's an all day event to get there. Mom used to take us into the city at least once a month. Dobbie, Libby, and I went to a movie last year."

"Do the three of you do things together often?" he asked.

"Who else is there? Sometimes I feel like their moderator, though. They bicker about the stupidest things." She saddled her horse and then Maggie's pony. He swung into the saddle and thought it didn't feel as painful this time. Maybe his muscles were becoming accustomed to the formation.

They rode in silence for a while and Will took in the beauty of the landscape. He had never seen anywhere more beautiful.

"I think I could live here forever," he said.

She gave him a wry smile. "Don't get attached, Ashley. We're not keeping you."

"I wasn't hinting. I have a life in Pittsburgh." A boring, vanilla existence with no horses, no stunning vistas, and no Anne.

"Do you have lots of friends?"

"Yes."

"And a girlfriend?"

"There was a girl I was seeing, but it wasn't serious and we haven't been in contact much since I left." He hadn't thought of her since he arrived and met Anne. He should probably call her and break it off officially.

"You said you've dated a lot of different girls, is that true?" Anne asked.

"Yes. Haven't you ever dated anyone besides Dobbie?"

She shook her head.

"Aren't you curious about what else is out there?" he asked.

She wouldn't look at him. He looked away and smiled. They reached what was presumably the east pasture. Dobbie was already there and rounding up the cows. He looked at Will in slight surprise, but nodded his head without comment. Will sat back to watch them work, and had to admit they worked well together. They didn't need words to communicate with each other, and each seemed to know what the other wanted done without having to ask. He watched the cows and couldn't help think their herd mentality was a lot like people; they were willing to follow a strong leader, no matter where he might take them. They didn't understand why their grazing was being disrupted, but they ambled together in a mass without much effort or protest. Some of them decided they wanted to graze on the way, but a few whistles and yells from Dobbie and Anne made them stop. Soon all three riders and the cows were heading to the west pasture.

"Where are the other hands and your father today?" Will asked. He had met the other hands, but they were like specters flitting unseen around the ranch.

"Dad went to a town a few hours away to look at some breeding stock. The hands are in the north and south pastures. We've had some trouble with the new calves, and they're checking for signs of coyotes or wolves."

Will nodded as if this made perfect sense to him. Everything on the ranch was a new and different experience. "If your dad decides to breed with the bull so many hours away, how do you, um, arrange a rendezvous with the cows here?"

Anne snorted a laugh and then put her hand over her mouth. "You're thinking too old school. We don't set them up for a blind date. We don't bring the bull here, only what we need to inseminate the female."

"You mean you actually…" He trailed off, unable to bring himself to say what he was picturing.

Anne nodded. "Squeamish yet?"

"Disturbed on a number of levels, but not squeamish. This totally ruins my image of the circle of life on a farm. I wouldn't have guessed you manipulated the system so much."

"When your livelihood depends on it you tend to take a less romantic and sentimental notion about things. Calving is too important to leave up to chance or luck. Plus the bulls get frisky and might damage the females." She squinted her eyes and looked at him. "Are you blushing, Ashley?"

"Maybe there are some parts of ranch life I would rather not know about," he said.

Anne chuckled and shook her head as they continued their slow walk. "We're branding next week. Do you think you can handle it?" she asked.

"People still brand?" He avoided the question with a question. He wasn't sure he wanted to see the cute little calves have a brand seared into their rumps.

"Of course we do. There are still thieves in the world, and even if no one stole there are fence breaks. Branding is the only legal way to identify cattle, along with ear tagging, but branding is the most recognizable."

"Don't you trust your neighbors?" He asked. In his imagination he was picturing warring ranchers stealing each other's cattle.

"The old motto says, 'Trust your neighbors, but still brand your livestock.'"

"I thought your neighbors are the great and mighty Henshaws," Will said.

"How do you think they got to be so great and mighty?" Anne asked. At Will's shocked look she hurried on. "They don't steal anymore, and I don't know that they ever did, but these ranches have been here for generations. Some rumors say the original Henshaws were rustlers and criminals, but I think that's conjecture and sour grapes because they're successful and wealthy."

"There are so many interesting stories here waiting to be told."

She looked at him in surprise. "Are you a writer?"

"Being a writer isn't practical. It doesn't pay the bills," he said.

"What a clever way of not answering my question," she said.

"Someone's persistent today. I enjoy writing. It's a good hobby, but as my dad reminds me often, it's not a practical career choice."

"Lots of people make their living writing full time," she pointed out.

He looked at her in surprise. "Suddenly you're the champion for an unconventional career?"

She smiled. "For you, not for me. You're free to do what you want with your life." Her smile died and her tone turned wistful.

He wanted to ask if ranching wasn't what she wanted to do with her life, but he didn't want to push her, and Dobbie wasn't too far away. Will wasn't sure if he was listening.

"Is anyone really free to do what he wants with his life?" Will asked. "Everyone has not only the practical responsibilities of everyday life, but also the pressure society and family put on us to live a certain way, or follow a certain path." Now he sounded wistful. Anne turned to look at him and something like understanding passed between them. Will's heart quickened in response to that look. There was something more to Anne than ranching, and he made it his goal to find out what it was.

He thought as he rode that he now had many goals concerning Anne. He wanted to find out her life's ambition. He wanted to make her open up and release her deep wells of emotion. He wanted to make her realize she wasn't in love with Dobbie and couldn't marry him. Most of all, he wanted to make her fall in love with him and convince her that somehow, someway, they would be together.

When they returned to the ranch they went their separate ways for a while. Anne had paperwork to do for the ranch, and Will headed to the kitchen for a snack. Libby was like a short order cook. She was always ready, willing, and able to feed whoever happened by at a moment's notice. Thankfully she had made a large batch of cookies and he grabbed a couple of those so she didn't feel the need to prepare food for him.

"You look deep in thought, Will," she said.

"I am."

She poured him some milk and sat down across from him. He looked at her in surprise. Libby almost never sat down. Besides Anne she was the hardest working girl he had ever seen.

"What's wrong with you?" he asked.

"I don't know." The despondency in her tone alarmed him. "Sometimes I feel sad and restless, and I don't know why."

Maybe because you're sixteen and doing the work of three grown women, or maybe because your sister is practically engaged to a man you have feelings for. Of course he didn't say any of that.

"Sometimes I feel that way, too," he said. He offered her one of his cookies, and they ate together in sympathetic silence.

CHAPTER 10

For the next few days things went smoothly at the ranch and Will began to hope he and Anne had turned a corner in their friendship. After the day he pulled the calf he went back to his tutoring duties, but in the evenings he and Anne spent time together talking and walking. Sometimes they were with Dobbie and Libby, but Anne was right; Dobbie and Libby bickered almost constantly about little and unimportant things. Dobbie was laid back and Libby was sweet natured. To see them at each other's throats only confirmed to Will they had unresolved and unrecognized feelings between them. What else could explain them acting so out of character with each other?

He wondered if all families were as oblivious as this one. If an outsider came to observe his family, would they learn things he didn't realize? Not only were Dobbie and Libby oblivious to their chemistry, but everyone else was oblivious to it, too. Anne seemed to find it normal that Dobbie sought out Libby whenever he came into the house. And there was more. Everyone was also oblivious to the building attraction between Anne and Will. Well, almost everyone. Libby watched them with a suspicious sort of interest, but she didn't comment on it.

As for Anne, Will was learning to recognize a pattern in her behavior. Every time she let her guard down and started to let him near the walls she had constructed around her heart she would immediately try to push him away and fortify her defenses. She was like a kitten that had been abused and needed to be coaxed into trusting humans again, only Anne's abuse had been self-inflicted. She had made herself the way she was because she thought it would help her do her duty, whatever she deemed that to be. He wasn't surprised when, after a few days of peace and friendship, she started to snap at him and avoid him again.

One day when he could take it no more, he stalked to the barn, determined to have it out with her. When he reached the barn, however, all thoughts of a confrontation fled as he took in the sight of Anne perched over a bull pen. The bull was agitated by her proximity and started to butt its head against the side of the pen. He was a large, mean bull, and if Anne fell in she wouldn't stand a chance. Before Will could think, he reacted by placing an arm around her waist and roughly jerking her off the side of the pen. She reacted in her normal manner by immediately flying into torrent of fists and feet.

"Let me go," she demanded.

"Stop acting like a wildcat and I will." He said it angrily because she had kicked his shin with her boots and it hurt.

She went limp in his arms, but then he didn't want to let her go for a different reason. It felt nice to hold her when she wasn't fighting him. Who was he kidding; it felt nice to hold her whatever state she was in.

"Are you going to let me go?" she asked, and the breathy quality of her voice betrayed her.

He let her go, but he didn't move away. She stayed where she was with her back almost touching his front. The tension between them made the air thick and he fought for a deep breath.

"Annie," he said, and laid a gentle hand on her waist. She turned and he put his other hand on the other side of her waist.

"Don't," she whispered. She looked up at him with large, pleading eyes that were almost his undoing. How could he not kiss her when she looked at him like that? Then he remembered Dobbie, and he refrained. He had no desire to be the cause of her cheating on a guy he liked and respected. He dropped his hands to his sides.

"What were you doing up there?" he asked.

"Changing a light bulb over the pen," she said.

That worked to bring him out of his attraction soaked haze somewhat. "Why were you doing that?"

"Because it needed to be done."

He put his hands on her shoulders and shook her slightly. "You're the foreman of this ranch. Delegate."

She shook him off. "Don't tell me how to run my ranch."

"I'm not. I'm telling you how not to get killed. Do you know how close you came to falling?"

"Do you know how many times I've done this before? You have no right to tell me what to do. You have no claim over me." Strangely that comment, though said by her, made her eyes well up with tears.

"Annie," he whispered again. He started to raise his hand to caress her face but she took a step back and pressed against the pen behind her.

"Don't. Go, just go."

He turned to go, and then she made an angry, frustrated sound and jumped on his back. She knocked him down and struggled to pin him there. As much as he wanted to show her up by pinning her to the ground again, he refused to give in to his baser desires. Instead he rolled over onto his back and pinned her arms down so she was lying on top of him.

"I pinned you," she said, and he laughed because she meant it.

"Let's look at the situation more objectively. Exactly who is pinning who?" He squeezed her arms to show her he had her pinned.

She glared at him and tried to hold her head up away from him, but after a while her neck gave out, and she laid her head on his chest.

"Stop fighting me," he said softly.

"I can't," she said. Her voice was full of fear.

"You can. I won't hurt you."

"You have no idea what you're already doing to me."

"Tell me."

"No."

"Annie," he pressed.

"Don't call me that," she said, but there was no anger in her tone.

"I will call you that, and I will make you open up to me."

"Don't, Will. Please, can't you see you have to leave me alone?"

"No, I don't see that at all. You need me."

"But you don't need me," she said.

"I want you. That's even better than needing," he said.

"You have an answer for everything," she said, irritation creeping back into her tone.

"I only wish that were true," he said. If he had an answer for everything, he would know how to get her away from Dobbie and make her his on a permanent basis. Thoughts of Dobbie made him feel guilty, and he knew he had to let her go. "If I release you will you stop trying to beat me up?"

She smiled against his chest. "For now."

He let her go, and they sat up. They sat on the floor of the barn, a foot away from each other, looking, but not touching.

"Why are you doing this to me?" she asked. "Why me? There are lots of girls."

He pressed his palm to her face, and she closed her eyes. *Because I'm falling in love with you,* he wanted to say, but of course he didn't. "There's no one else like you, Annie."

"I'm a novelty to you," she said, and when she opened her eyes they were sad. "A freakish phenomenon, and once you figure me out, you'll lose interest and go away."

He shook his head. "You're like a rare gemstone. You sparkle differently in all types of light, and I don't think I'll ever get tired of looking at you."

"There's only one type of light for me, and this is it. This is all I'll ever be, a country girl with a high school education."

He put his other hand on her face to cup it. "Tell me what you want, and I'll do my best to make it happen, Annie."

She shook her head as well as she could while it was encased in his hands. "You're not a magician, Will, and that's what it will take. There's no use talking about what could be, or what might have been."

"Trust me," he whispered. "Tell me."

Her eyes were tortured as she studied him. Could she trust him with her secret? She wanted to, but she was afraid. She opened her mouth to speak, and then they heard hooves pounding in the yard. The moment was over. Anne closed the doors to her heart, brushed Will's hands aside, stood, and walked away.

$\mathcal{A}$nne tried to push Will away again after the episode in the barn, but he wouldn't let her. Every time she tried to avoid him, he found a way to be with her, even if it meant involving Libby and Dobbie in his schemes. One night he asked them to go to dinner and a movie in Billings.

"Like a double date?" Dobbie asked. He looked between Will and Libby with a suspicious frown.

"Not a date for us," Libby said. "Will and I are friends." Dobbie's face relaxed until she continued. "Maybe I'll meet someone interesting there."

"You're not meeting a stranger in Billings," Dobbie said, then realized she was teasing and picked her up under his arm and twirled her around. "Libby, you're a menace."

Will almost rolled his eyes. As the days progressed he found it more difficult to hold his tongue. It wasn't his business, he told himself over and over again. He was even more convinced of that fact when he learned something as soon as they arrived in Billings.

"Libby, if I pay for you tonight, does it count as a birthday gift?" Dobbie asked.

"If your conscience will allow it," Libby replied.

"When is your birthday?" Will asked her.

"In two weeks," Libby said.

"And you'll be seventeen?" he asked.

She shook her head. "I'll be sixteen. We get so used to being two years apart that when Anne turned eighteen we all started saying I was sixteen, I guess."

Will's eyes bugged. "You're only fifteen."

"Wow, you really are good at math," Anne said.

He tipped her hat over her face. He couldn't believe Libby was only fifteen. She was so mature for her age. Probably because she handled much more than any girl her age ever should. At any rate, it was too early for her to have a romance with anyone. He redoubled his efforts to remain silent on the Dobbie situation. He had no intention of heaping one more thing on her head she wasn't ready to deal with. Their family situation was heartily unfair. Anne and Libby both grew up too fast and still shouldered too much responsibility. He wished there was something he could do to change it.

"What's wrong, frowny face?" This came from Anne.

"Frowny face? Are you heavily medicated?" he asked.

"My euphoria over a night off is tampering with my sensibilities. You still didn't answer my question."

"I'm thinking deep thoughts. Sometimes it happens. Don't be concerned; I'll be annoying you again in no time."

"Who said you're not annoying me now?" she asked, and she was only half teasing. He was exasperating when he was talking incessantly, but at least she knew what he was thinking. His silences drove her insane. *She* was supposed to be the silent one, not him.

Will would have put her in a headlock, but he couldn't do that in front of Dobbie. Dobbie may not be in love with Anne, but he had a strongly protective and possessive nature. If he realized Will was invading his territory, he wouldn't react well. Will might be able to take Anne, but he was no match for Dobbie. They were equal in height, but like Matt Chapman, Dobbie looked like he was sculpted from marble. He thought of Anne's statement that muscles formed at the gym couldn't compete with those formed by doing real work.

"Why are you so quiet?" Anne asked, and now she was irritated.

He realized his silence was bothering her and smiled. "I was actually thinking you were right about something you said."

"What?" she asked.

"Wouldn't you like to know," he said.

She narrowed her eyes at him. "Don't make me take you down again, Ashley."

"You have a creative memory, Annie."

"You girls go on to the restaurant, and we'll meet you there," Dobbie said, surprising them all. "Will and I have something to do."

Will felt a slight current of fear. Was Dobbie finally picking up on the tension between Anne and him? Was he going to confront him right here in the middle of Billings?

Anne and Libby sauntered off toward the restaurant arm in arm. For a moment Dobbie and Will watched them go. Will was thinking what a pretty pair they were, and he wondered if Dobbie thought the same thing.

"I'm not sure two sisters have ever been so different," Will commented.

"You've got that right," Dobbie said. He turned around and walked the way they came. "Thanks for letting me use you as my cover. I need to buy something for Libby's birthday present, but if I went alone, Anne would plague me with questions. She doesn't question what you tell her."

Will followed him into a fancy kitchen supply store on a side street. The store looked like something Libby would love. Dobbie already knew what he wanted to purchase and went straight to a pretty and delicate tea pot. "Can you believe they make something so useless?" he asked, but he smiled when he bought it.

"What did you get Anne for her birthday?" Will asked and almost laughed as he waited for the answer. Dobbie didn't disappoint.

"A new calf jack. Anne's too down to earth for anything frilly like this." He sounded both relieved and disappointed. He might never admit it, but Will guessed he liked having someone to buy girly things for.

Will knew Anne would have liked something feminine, too. He wondered if it hurt her that Dobbie bought her something practical while he bought her sister something pretty. Then he decided she probably didn't notice the difference. He wondered how she would react if he did the same thing. Instead of finding out he did the opposite. He bought dish towels for Libby and a pretty coffee mug for Anne. He noticed she drank coffee every morning, but didn't have her own special mug. It wasn't her birthday, but he didn't care. She deserved something pretty and feminine, all of her own. If Dobbie thought it was curious another man was buying his girlfriend a present, he didn't comment, but then he was too wrapped up in excitement over his present to notice.

The bags were plain brown paper and they kept the girls guessing where they had been through much of dinner. Dobbie and Anne kept Will and Libby amused by telling stories of happenings on the ranch.

"Remember when you got your head stuck in the calf chute?" Anne asked.

Dobbie groaned. "I'll never forget it, or the blistering lecture your dad gave me afterwards."

"You never told him I was the one who dared you to do it," Anne said affectionately.

"I should have known better than to listen to you. You always got me into trouble, but I couldn't resist trying to prove you wrong. Someday I suppose maybe I'll finally succeed in doing so."

"That's a pleasant thought for you," Anne said. "Like a happy fairy tale."

"I guess you guys will have a lot to tell your kids," Will said. Libby choked on a sip of her soda, and Anne thumped her on the back. An awkward silence descended on the table, and for some reason it made Will angry. Maybe because it followed stories of all the time Anne and Dobbie had spent together. "Haven't you ever talked about your future children?" he continued. "I mean, you've been dating for four years. Everyone tells me it's inevitable you'll be married some day. I would think it would be a natural part of your relationship to talk about the future."

"We do talk about the future," Anne said. She, too, sounded angry.

"What do you have planned?" Will said. "If you don't mind my asking."

"We're going to expand the ranch," Dobbie said, and then started naming off a long list of things he and Anne wanted to do to the ranch.

Will gave Anne a surreptitious glance, and she glared at him in return. He knew she was aware of his thoughts. Dobbie didn't mention one word about marriage, love, or children. It was all about the business.

"Hadn't we better go so we can make our movie?" Libby asked.

"Sure," Will agreed. He felt bad he had made a fifteen year old play peacemaker.

They paired off on their walk to the movie theater. They had taken the train into Billings, so they were limited by where they could go. Libby walked with Will, and Anne walked with Dobbie. When Will glanced behind him, he saw them clasping hands, and the sight made him sad.

"Are you feeling bad because you're old, Will?" Libby asked with a mischievous smile.

He put his arm around her shoulders. "No, but I'm feeling bad you're so young, Libby."

"Why? Because now you're really certain you're too old for me?" She put her arm around his waist.

"Yes, that's exactly why. All these weeks it's only your age and not our total lack of attraction to each other that has been holding me back." He squeezed her shoulders. "I feel badly that you have so much on your little shoulders."

"I'm happy."

"Are you really?" he asked. She certainly did her duty without complaint, but that didn't necessarily equal happiness.

"Mostly. Sometimes I wonder what else is out there, but it's not like I can leave."

"If you could, would you?"

She thought about that for a while. "Only if Anne went first. I couldn't leave her here. She would kill herself trying to do everything."

"She'll have Dobbie to help her," Will said. His grip tightened on her shoulder, and she gave him a knowing smile.

"They're two of a kind. Anne wouldn't know what to do in the house all day."

"So you're saying if Anne left Dobbie could take over her duties and you would be free to leave someday, too," Will said.

"I suppose, but it's a moot point. Anne is more committed to the ranch than she is even to Dobbie. It's in her blood. She'll never leave."

Will wasn't sure about that, but he wasn't ready to share what he had been thinking about. "What do you want in a man?" he asked instead.

"I want someone cultured, educated, and sensitive." She said it with all the certainty of her fifteen years, as if she had thought about it beforehand and had a predetermined answer.

"You're very young. Maybe your taste will change," he suggested.

"Why should it? If I can't find what I want then I'll stay single and keep house for Dad. I'm happy doing that."

It wasn't right that a young girl should be cynical about her future prospects. "Libby, you're sweet and pretty and talented. You'll find someone great."

She squeezed his waist. "Maybe I'll come to Pittsburgh in a couple of years and you can fix me up."

"I don't think I would risk Dobbie's wrath that way," Will said.

Libby was instantly irritated. "What does he have to do with it?"

More than you know, Will wanted to say. Even now he could feel Dobbie's eyes boring into the back of his head. "He's protective of you."

"I suppose all future brothers-in-law are that way."

"Maybe so," he said, but didn't believe a word.

nne felt like she was suffocating. If there was one thing she wasn't, it was stupid. Of course she knew what Will was doing. He was preventing her from escaping him, and it was having his desired effect. He was who she thought of when she woke, before she went to bed, and all the time in between. She had thought when Dobbie and the other cowboys returned, the contrast between him and them would make her loathe him, but it didn't work. To her surprise, he was coming out on top. Had Dobbie always been so reserved and insensitive to her needs and feelings?

She suppressed a groan. She couldn't be thinking these thoughts and having these feelings, whatever they were. The "double date" with Libby only made it worse. Did Dobbie really only view their relationship as a business merger? No, of course not. He wouldn't do that to her, at least not on purpose. He wouldn't marry her if he didn't love her, would he? Maybe he, like her, didn't know the difference. He had never dated anyone else, either. How were they to know if what they had was true love or not? Surely true love was what you felt for your best friend of many years, and not some stranger you had only known for a few weeks. Besides, Will was all wrong for her, wasn't he?

She was confused, and the almost constant amount of time she spent with Will was making it worse. She had to get away, had to get some space to think. If she could only get some time to herself, she was sure she could push him from her mind and heart. He was opening doors and windows inside her that couldn't be allowed to stay open. If he made her feel the things she was trying so hard to suppress, then she would spend the rest of her life regretting what might have been. There was no doubt in her mind that he would leave here and forget all about her. He was from the city. He had lots of friends and girlfriends. He couldn't maintain a lasting interest in a loner country girl.

Unfortunately all these thoughts coincided with one of the most important social events of their summer: the fourth of July. Every year their family joined the other neighbors at the Henshaw's ranch. Not only did the entire family attend, but all the ranch hands, too. They emptied the stables because the hands rode their horses to the party while the family drove in their two trucks. Anne would have preferred to ride her horse so she could make a hasty retreat, but that would have sent the wrong message to her neighbors. Here in the country they still observed the lines of wealth and lineage. The landowners rode in the car while the employees rode on their horses. The only exception to this rule was Dobbie, but he had once been a landowner before his parents died and their ranch house burned down. After that her father bought the small plot of land and put the money in a trust for Dobbie. He was eighteen now and could access the trust. She wondered what he would do with it. She wondered if he would consult her. Sometimes it was difficult for her to fathom that she and Dobbie would one day be married and have their lives joined completely. No one was around, but she blushed anyway. She definitely couldn't think of Dobbie that way yet. Maybe those feelings and desires appeared after marriage. She hoped so, or they were in big trouble.

"Libby, can I borrow a dress?"

Anne was distracted when she asked her sister, so it took her a minute to realize Libby had dropped a watermelon on the counter at the request.

"You want to what a what?" Libby asked.

"I've worn dresses before," Anne said, annoyed.

"I wasn't alive when you were christened in church," Libby said. She eyed her sister speculatively. "What's brought on this sudden interest in dresses?"

"I am a female of this species, contrary to popular opinion. Occasionally I would like to take off my chaps and look like one."

Libby was still eyeing her, but in a critical way Anne knew meant she was sizing her up and trying to figure out the proper dress.

"We're not the same style," Libby said at last. "None of my dresses would work on you." Anne started to protest, but Libby hurried on. "Mom has one that will be perfect."

Anne swallowed hard. "Mom's dress?"

Libby nodded. She took her sister's hand and led her to her bedroom. By now they had gotten rid of almost all her mother's clothes, but Libby had retained anything classic and timeless. She had an eye for fashion and so had her mother. Although, their taste wasn't always the same. Now Libby rooted around in the back of her closet until she located a simple brown silk dress that could have been made today or twenty years ago.

"Try it on," Libby commanded and stood back to watch her sister's transformation. She whistled appreciatively. "My sister cleans up well."

Anne smiled shyly, and Libby hid her own smile. Will Ashley certainly was having an interesting effect on her tomboyish, taciturn sister.

"Let me do your hair and makeup," Libby said.

"Okay." Anne agreed more readily than Libby imagined. Maybe there was more to her than Libby even knew, and she thought she knew everything about her. She had been watching the slowly budding relationship between Anne and Will with fascination and trepidation. A part of her she didn't understand was rooting for Will, but she didn't want any of them to get hurt. Dobbie would be crushed, and as much as he plagued her sometimes she didn't want that.

"Anne," Libby said gently. "Be careful, all right?"

"What do you mean?"

"You know what I mean. Be careful. I like Will, but he's older, and more experienced, and temporary. You and Dobbie are forever."

Anne turned away from her to look in the mirror. "I don't know what you're talking about, Libby. Nothing is going on between me and Will. We're not even friends, really. We're nothing alike, and he drives me crazy. You know the type of guy I like, and you know the life I want."

Libby studied her reflection in the mirror. "I used to know those things. I'm not sure I do anymore."

Anne's frown deepened. "There's nothing there. There can't be." Her tone took on some desperation, and Libby stood to put her arm around her shoulders.

"It'll be okay," she said soothingly. "It will all work out. It always does."

"You're a hopeless romantic, you know it, little Elizabeth? If your queen had been like you she wouldn't have died a virgin."

Libby smiled. All the sisters sometimes teased each other about their namesake queens. "Maybe she was a romantic, and that's why she never married. She was looking for Mr. Right, and he never showed up."

Anne put her finger down her throat and made a gagging sound. "Get me out of here before this romanticism becomes contagious."

"Come on. I'll do your hair and makeup now."

"Don't make me look gaudy," Anne said and then wished she could take the words back when Libby stopped and froze her with a look.

"Do you really think I'm capable of such a thing?" Libby asked.

Anne studied her sister's calf-length flared dress, embroidered handkerchief, and French twist hairdo. "No, you're not capable of such a thing."

Satisfied, Libby turned back toward the bathroom and led Anne behind her.

It's all going to be worth it, Anne told herself over and over. She had thought the pain of rope burn was bad, but it was nothing compared to having her eyebrows ripped out with tweezers. Libby insisted on a full makeover including brows, manicure, and pedicure.

"No one is even going to see my toes," Anne protested.

"But you'll know they're pretty, and it will make you feel good," Libby said.

Anne growled. "Nothing makes sense in your world, Libby."

"And yet you willingly volunteered to enter it. I guess that makes you crazy," Libby said. Despite Anne's complaints she was enjoying the time with her sister. They were close, but by choice and not by circumstance. Anne was right; they lived in two different worlds that didn't intersect much. Anne was always outdoors doing hard, manual labor, while Libby worked indoors doing whatever domestic work needed done. Except for supper each night and church on Sundays, they didn't even see each other much. Sometimes Libby felt like she saw Dobbie more than she saw her sister, but she blamed that on his voracious appetite. He was always hanging around the kitchen, begging for a bite. Like a puppy. She smiled. She would have to tell him that. It would make him furious. Having Will there for the summer was like a dream come true. Besides Dobbie he was the only person who ever stayed around the kitchen to talk to her. He was fascinating company, like a real big brother, and she found herself dreading the day he would be out of their lives.

"You're quiet all of a sudden," Anne said. She sounded irritable. "Is this a game you and Ashley play to drive me crazy?"

Libby smiled. "I was thinking about him, actually, and about how sad it will be when he leaves. He's changed us somehow. It feels more like home with him here. It's like he soothes over all the hurts."

"There are no hurts," Anne said. "You're dwelling too much on your blasted feelings. Everything is fine in our family the way it is. Will is interfering where he shouldn't, and it's only going to cause heartache after he leaves."

"Will isn't interfering, he's helping. You should hear Maggie spouting all the math facts she's learned. She sounds like Kitty. And Kitty is so euphoric she hasn't stopped smiling since he arrived. He talked her home school advisor into letting her advance her classes this year. And I actually feel qualified to take the SAT now, although I might have to have someone snapping beans beside me to trigger my memory."

"What?" Anne said.

"Nothing. The point is, Will is doing us all a lot of good, and you need to go easier on him."

"I've been very nice to him lately," Anne said.

"Then why did I hear you ask Kitty to look up all the ways to take down a man who is bigger than you?"

Anne's eyes narrowed. "That's between me and him. I have a score to settle, but it's beside the point. I've been the soul of courtesy to him lately."

"Yes, polite and distant courtesy. You know that's not what he wants from you."

"I can't give him what he wants."

"Can't you?" Libby asked.

"Elizabeth," Anne exclaimed. "You're the one who is always telling me to be nicer to Dobbie and pay him more attention. Now you're telling me to cheat on him?"

"I'm telling you no such thing. If you want to be with Will, then break up with Dobbie, and do it gently. You're not married to him yet. You have the right to choose another man."

"Will doesn't want me," Anne said sadly. "He's bored and lonely and out of his element. I'm an interesting distraction and a challenge. As soon as he leaves here at the end of the summer, he'll forget all about me."

Libby wasn't sure about that, but it was between the two of them. She had never been a meddler, and she had no plans to start. "Don't hurt Dobbie, okay?"

"I'll never understand you in a million years, even if you are the closest person on earth to me," Anne said. "Dobbie makes you crazy, I know he does. Yet you're more worried about his feelings than anyone else's."

"I've told you why a million times. We're all he has. We're his only family. He needs us."

"He's fine. If there's anyone more of a self-sufficient loner than me, it's Dobbie. I could dump him tomorrow, and he would dust himself off and walk away unscathed."

Libby shook her head. "You're wrong."

"Lib, he's been my boyfriend for four years. Which one of us do you think knows him better?"

Libby shrugged but didn't reply. Anne threw up her hands in frustration. She would have stalked from the room, but then she remembered she needed Libby to apply her makeup and finish her hair, so she sat meekly in the chair and worked to keep her mouth shut.

Will couldn't believe he was actually attending a real live social event at the ranch. As far as he could tell, the grownups (and by grownups he was including Libby) worked all day while Kitty studied and Maggie played. They fell into bed at night exhausted from their labors and got up the next morning to start all over again. He had never met people who worked harder. The only break they took was Sunday church, and, even after that, Libby still had to cook lunch and clean up while Anne, Dobbie, and Matt tended to the animals.

But now it was all about to change, at least for this one day. Like he had hoped it would be, July fourth was a huge event in the community, and it was celebrated with as much fanfare as their forefathers probably celebrated. On top of all that, he was finally going to get to meet the fabled Henshaws.

He didn't think his enthusiasm for the day could get any higher, and then he saw her. Anne descended the stairs and everything came to a standstill. She was out of her chaps and minus her Stetson, and she was beautiful. Unfortunately, he wasn't the only one who noticed. Dobbie dropped the newspaper and stood, too.

"Anne, you look as pretty as a newborn calf," he said with some reverence.

"Thank you," Anne said, and a pretty blush lit her cheeks.

"You blush?" Dobbie asked. "I had no idea." He grinned at her and dodged the pillow she threw at him.

Behind her came Libby and Dobbie grew silent again. Will thought Libby looked pretty, too. While Anne's hair was brown with blond streaks, Libby's had auburn highlights. She wore a white sundress, and she looked fresh and feminine.

"All that's missing is a daisy in your hair," Will said. He went forward, took Libby's hand, and bowed.

"You may rise," she said royally.

"Cheeky," he said, and winked at her. When they turned around Dobbie and Anne were both scowling at them. Will ignored them and squeezed Libby's hand. "Can you dance?"

"Yes, can you?" she said.

"Guess," he said, and she smiled a secret little smile that let him know she was onto his game.

"We can all dance," Anne said irritably. "No need to dwell on it."

They helped Libby load what seemed like dozens of containers of food into the truck.

"I've never seen so much food in my life," Will said. "What do you do with the leftovers?"

The others laughed. "There won't be leftovers. We're feeding cowboys," Anne said.

Will was doubtful, and his doubts increased when they arrived and saw several long tables strung together and laden down with even more food. Then he took a look around at the many, many cowboys surrounding him and began to fear they might not have enough. Some of the cowhands made Dobbie and Matt look like saplings in comparison. He noticed a young man eying him from across the room, and the look he was giving was less than friendly. From the quality of his clothes and the way he carried himself, Will guessed him to be Marcus Henshaw, the heir to this vast fortune. And it *was* vast. It made the Chapman ranch look like someone's back yard with three times the number of barns and what looked like millions of cattle. Will began to feel uncomfortable toward Marcus and sent a few of his own glares to the man. He must be interested in Anne and sense Will was some sort of competition for her.

It took a while for his jealousy to clear enough for him to realize the not-so-subtle glances Marcus was darting weren't aimed at Anne; they were aimed at Libby. No wonder he was upset with Will, he must have assumed he and Libby really were on a date. Will almost smiled in relief. One less competitor for Anne. On the other hand, Libby was only fifteen, and he had been told Marcus was twenty, like him. That was too old, so he linked his arm through Libby's and didn't give Marcus the chance to approach. Libby gave him an odd look, but waited to speak until they were alone.

"You're playing with fire, Will," she said.

He gave her a puzzled look.

"Using me to make my sister jealous," she said.

"I'm not," he protested. "Okay, maybe I was a little bit back at the house, but I promise I'm not, Libby. I'm saving you."

She smiled. "For what?"

"Not for what, from what, or rather whom."

"Your convoluted grammar lost me," she said.

"Marcus Henshaw is interested in you."

She giggled a sweet, girlish laugh. "That's funny."

He shook his head. "I'm not kidding. I know these things."

She patted his arm. "That's very big brotherly of you to be protective of me, but you needn't worry. Marcus is in college. He dates lots of different girls, and he is possibly the most eligible man in Montana. Everyone everywhere knows about his family's wealth, and he's what you might call 'a catch.' Believe me when I tell you he has no interest in a sheltered fifteen-year-old neighbor." She nervously smoothed her hand over her perfectly coiffed hair. Will gave her a look.

"A girl likes to look her best in all situations," she said peevishly. "Honestly, Will, don't turn into Dobbie. He's always imagining the young cow hands have a crush on me."

Most likely they did, he thought. She was young, but she was pretty and sweet, and an amazing cook. If a man were determined to be with her he would easily overlook her young age. "Libby, did it ever occur to you that you're what's called 'a catch?'"

She giggled again. "Oh, Will, I'm going to miss you when you go away." Impulsively she threw her arms around him and gave him an affectionate squeeze.

He smiled and returned her hug. "And I'm going to miss you, little Libby." She was like a real little sister to him in so many ways. He had always wanted a little sister to be friends with and tell secrets to, and Libby fit the bill perfectly. Of course the rest of the room had no idea their affection for each other was purely platonic, and more than one person was seething at the sight.

He filtered through the long line of food alone because Libby helped Mrs. Henshaw serve. It made him slightly sad she didn't get a day off from her duties, but like always, she didn't seem to mind. He thought he filled his plate to the maximum, but when he sat across from Dobbie and Matt, he realized his plate looked like a snack to them.

"Aren't you hungry?" Anne asked with a smirk.

"I'm watching my girlish figure," he replied. He wouldn't let her get to him, not today when they were supposed to be having fun.

She stole his dinner roll. "I don't figure you'll miss it, and Libby makes the best."

"Give that back," he said and lunged for it. She held it behind her over her head and he pinned her to him to reach it.

The tension between them was instant and palpable, and they both realized they were in public and most likely being watched. Anne handed him the roll and faced forward.

"Thanks," Will said politely and then, for lack of anything better to do, split the roll, buttered it, and ate it. He surreptitiously glanced around, but no one seemed to have found the interaction odd, at least no one in the immediate area. At the next table over, Marcus Henshaw was watching and smiling to himself.

After the meal, Libby was stuck with the cleanup. Dobbie and Matt sauntered off with the other men to play horseshoes, so Will asked Anne to go for a walk.

"I don't know," she said uncertainly, and he was annoyed by her reluctance.

"I promise not to make a pass at you. We can take a chaperone if you don't feel safe, Miss Chapman."

"All right, Ashley, don't get your feathers in a whirl," she said.

He smiled and his anger evaporated. "I love hearing all your charming colloquialisms."

"Don't you have any in Pittsburgh?" she asked.

"Does, 'Yo, get your hands off my pierogi!' count?"

She laughed even though she had no idea what a pierogi was. "What's a pierogi?"

"Pittsburgh has lots of Italian and Polish descendants. A pierogi is a Polish pasta with mashed potatoes stuffed inside the dough."

"I'm not as into food as Libby is, but that sounds good," she said.

"They're amazing. Especially with cheese, caramelized onions and kielbasa."

"Kielbasa?"

"It's a type of sausage. Have you ever been east of the Mississippi?"

She shook her head. The slight sadness was back.

"Visit me," he said.

"How would I explain that to Dad and Dobbie?"

She had a point, but he didn't want to let the idea go. The thought of Anne with him in Pittsburgh was intoxicating. "We're friends. Aren't you allowed to visit friends? You can stay with my parents to make it legit. I live on campus, so I won't even be sleeping there."

She smiled, but it still looked sad. "It must be nice in the world where you and Libby live. Do puppies ride unicorns and gold coins fall from the sky?"

He smiled, too, even though she was mocking him. "Yes, but they're all made of chocolate, so you can't really buy anything."

"Pessimist," she accused.

"Did you know Marcus Henshaw has a thing for Libby?" he asked.

"Sure. He's had a crush on her for a while now. All boys like Libby.

She's pretty and feminine and they all want to rescue her while eating her delicious food. She's like a drug to men."

"You're jealous," he said.

"A little."

He was surprised she admitted it. "Why would you be jealous of Libby? You're beautiful, and capable, and smart, and funny, and I'm going to stop now because I'm embarrassing myself."

She surprised him again by linking her arm through his. "Even if that was a line, I'm going to fall for it and be flattered."

"It wasn't a line, Annie. You know how I feel about you."

"I know how you think you feel, but you'll be gone soon, back to your normal life and your normal type of girl." The hint of sadness was back in her tone.

He squeezed her arm. "I'll never forget you, Anne, and I'll compare every girl I meet from now on to you, and the worst part is they'll all come up lacking."

She looked away from him and sniffled. He had to force himself not to smile. It was a heady feeling to know he was the only one with whom she cried. He stopped and looked around. They were out in the open but so far from the festivities that they were out of view, so he took her in his arms and crushed her to him while she cried.

"You look so beautiful," he said.

"Do you like me better in a dress?" she said between sobs and hiccups.

"I like you in everything I've seen you wear. I didn't know they made chaps for girls, and I didn't know a girl could make chaps look so good. You should be their spokesmodel."

For some reason his words made her cry harder, and he wondered if it was possible she was crying happy tears for once. He wanted to tell her he loved her, but he couldn't. Not when she wasn't his. Her tears came to an end, but she didn't pull away. If anything, she snuggled further into his embrace.

"Will," she whispered.

"What?" He whispered, too.

"I..." She tightened her grip on him. "We should get back."

He nodded and kissed the top of her head before letting her go. She took a couple of steps back, and they stood looking at each other until the tension became unbearable.

"Annie, I want so many things when I'm with you. I didn't know it was possible to feel so much so soon."

She blinked at him and her large eyes looked even more luminous. "I thought you were the expert on feelings."

"Only on the ones I've already had. Everything is new with you." He brushed the back of his hand down her cheek.

"How do I know what you're telling me is real? How do I know it isn't some line you've used a thousand times?" she asked.

"You'll have to follow your heart," he said.

"I don't know how to do that. I stopped listening to my heart a long time ago," she said.

"We'll figure it out together. It will be okay. It will work out somehow."

She smiled.

"What?"

"That's what Libby said."

He smiled, too. "Smart girl, your sister."

Far away they heard the sound of laughter and reluctantly turned and walked back to the party.

CHAPTER 14

When they returned to the barn where the party was being held, they found the space in the middle of the room had been cleared and a speaker system was being set up.

"There really is dancing here," Will said.

"There really is."

He looked around. Besides the four Chapman girls, there was one other young girl who Anne said was Kitty's best friend, Cecily. Cecily's mother wasn't present, so the only other woman there was Mrs. Henshaw. Meanwhile, there were about seventy five cowboys in attendance.

"Your dance card is going to be very full," Will said.

She shook her head. "Things are different here. Ranchers get first dibs on the females. And you'll take precedent since you're our guest. Plus we do a lot of line dances and no one needs a partner for those."

"You actually rank dance partners by their social status?" he asked.

"Don't sound so appalled," she said. "It's part of a social system that works very well. You may notice there is a vast shortage of females here. If we had no system to deal with the shortage it could get out of hand. This way the cowboys know they pretty much don't have a chance, and they keep to themselves and don't get their hopes up.

Sometimes I dance with some of our older hands who are like family, but it's like dancing with an uncle."

He tried to absorb what she said and not react. He had to remind himself again things were different here. They didn't play by the same rules he was used to, and, as she said, they had their reasons. He supposed there was also a safety factor involved in keeping the girls out of reach of the cowhands. If they were viewed as accessible, they might become targets for unwanted attention. He had already learned from Dobbie a few of their cowhands had things in their past they would rather keep quiet, such as criminal records. Some of their helpers came and stayed forever, like family, while others drifted from ranch to ranch working for wages until they got bored and left. Those were the ones who needed to be watched, but with so few qualified workers available, it was a case of taking what you could get.

The first song was a line dance. Will had never heard a country song before, let alone tried to dance to one. He was out of his element as usual, but this time Anne was a patient teacher, and only laughed at him a few times. When the music switched to a slow dance Dobbie came to claim Anne.

"Come on, Anne, they're playing our song," he said, and then led her away.

Will was content to sit one out, but Libby approached him. "Time to prove your dancing skills," she said.

He smiled, took her hand, and started to dance. "Are you having fun?"

"Yes," she said. "Are you?"

"Yes," he said, and darted a glance at Anne and Dobbie.

"Try to be a little more subtle, Will," Libby said seriously. "The last thing we need is gossip, and cowboys love to tell tales."

"I'll try, but she doesn't make it easy. She blows so hot and cold I never know where I stand with her. She's making me crazy."

"If it's any consolation I think you're having the same effect on her," Libby said.

Will pulled her slightly closer. "Why? What did she say about me?"

"I said cowboys tell tales, not me. I don't blab confidences," she said.

"Fine, then I won't tell you what I heard about Marcus Henshaw and you."

"Not fair, Will. I have to live here forever. You get to go away. You have to tell me everything you know."

"I know he's heading this way right now and about to cut in," he said.

"Very funny," she said, and then froze in shock when she felt a tap on her shoulder.

"May I cut in?" Marcus asked politely.

Will suppressed a smile and handed Libby over.

When he turned, he noticed Anne was alone again, and he reclaimed her before anyone else could. "Where's Dobbie?" he asked.

"Talking shop with Mr. Henshaw."

They danced in silence for a while as he surveyed the dance floor. All the eligible girls were dancing, even Maggie.

"Who's that boy dancing with Maggie?"

"Mathew Henshaw," Anne said. "He's Kitty's age, but I think he's developing a crush on Maggie. Don't worry, she's completely oblivious to him unless he's holding a snake or something else she finds interesting."

"Does everyone marry their neighbor here?" he asked.

"Proximity works wonders," she said. "Who else is there? And who better to marry than someone you've known your whole life?"

"Oh, I don't know. Maybe someone you are actually in love with," he said, and she stiffened. "Hypothetically speaking," he added, and she relaxed. Dobbie didn't come back for a long time, so Will and Anne kept dancing.

He pulled out all the stops to impress her, and hoped he was succeeding. He placed a hand on her back and used it to spin her away from him and pull her back. When he looked around, though, everyone seemed to know how to dance. Strange a place with so much testosterone would also breed such good dancers. Everything was backwards here. He felt like Alice through the looking glass.

Anne gave a little sigh of satisfaction, and it pulled him back to the moment. She felt right in his arms, like she belonged and they were made for each other. He was glad they were a physical fit, if nothing else.

There was so much he wanted to say, but for once he didn't know how to say it. So he kept silent and tried to quash down his raging emotions. At last Dobbie returned, and when he did, he was angry. Will saw the angry look on his face and readied a defense, but then Dobbie spoke, and he had to fight off his amusement.

"How could you let Libby dance with Marcus?" he asked. "He's too old for her."

"He's my age," Will pointed out.

"You're too old for her, but at least I can keep a constant eye on you. Him I don't trust." He stared as he watched Libby and Marcus twirl around the dance floor. They made a striking pair, and Will said as much.

Dobbie's scowl intensified. "She's fifteen. He's twenty. That's not acceptable." He turned to Anne. "I'm going to have to do something about this. Do you mind dancing with him a while longer?"

"I'll manage," Anne said, and then she and Will stopped dancing to watch the drama that was about to unfold. Dobbie stalked over to Marcus and Libby and angrily demanded to cut in. Marcus wasn't happy about it, but there was no graceful way to say no, so he handed her over. At first Libby and Dobbie danced in silence, but then his temper must have boiled over because he said something to her, she stomped on his foot, and fled the barn. He threw an apologetic look to Anne and Will and hobbled after Libby.

"Doesn't it bother you when he does that?" Will asked.

"What? Protect my sister? Why should it bother me? Marcus is too old and too experienced for her."

"You don't think he seemed overly angry at the guy for dancing with her?" Will asked.

"Marcus, Dobbie, and I have had a rivalry together that dates back to our days at the fair. I got over it, but Dobbie never did. He's had a dislike of Marcus for a while now and seeing him dance with Libby gave him reason to act on it."

"There are none so blind as those who will not see," Will said, shaking his head when Anne gave him a questioning look. "Never mind. The less said by me on this subject, the better."

After dancing came the fireworks. Will's idea of someone who did their own fireworks included a couple of Roman candles and some sparklers, but he forgot everything was bigger in Montana. The display the Henshaws put on rivaled anything he had ever seen in Pittsburgh and must have cost a fortune. They were so grand he wished for his cell phone so he could take a picture. Anne sat beside him on a blanket. He so badly wanted to put his arm around her, but he didn't. Instead he inched his hand toward her and barely caressed the edge of her hand. She made a small move toward him, and they linked pinkies. He thought if he lived to be a hundred, it would be the sweetest hand holding experience he would ever have.

Dobbie and Libby never returned. Will didn't find out what happened to them until the car ride home, and by then they had made up and were laughing. Libby had hay in her hair and Will wondered if they had been kissing, but then he learned that she saw him come after her and hid in a hay mound until a mouse ran over her leg and she screamed and jumped up. When she did, she frightened Dobbie who grabbed a nearby pitchfork and came within an inch of spearing her. His fear for her safety made him angry, and they got into another argument until she ran off and hid somewhere else. By the time he found her they were both over their anger and they ended up playing hide and seek for the rest of the evening.

"You played hide and seek at the Henshaw's?" Anne asked, incredulous.

"Yes, and it was the most fun ever," Libby enthused. "They have so many places to hide, and we weren't familiar with them all like we are at our house." She and Dobbie launched into another fit of laughter over something. They sounded like little kids, and Will was glad. Libby had taken up the reins of adulthood when she was ten years old, and Dobbie when he was fourteen. If there were ever two people who needed to act like little kids it was these two. He looked at Anne and guessed she was thinking the same thing. She could do with more silliness and laughter in her life, too. Maybe he would work to make it happen. He sat back and added one more thing to the long list of goals he had compiled surrounding Anne Chapman.

CHAPTER 15

For days after July Fourth, Will was lost in his own world, thinking. Anne was holding something back, he was sure. And no matter what he tried, she wouldn't open up to him and confess what it was. Whatever it was, he was sure it held the key to her future, and as the days drew closer to his departure, he became more desperate to figure out her secret. A week after the party, he received help from an unlikely source.

"Did you hear?" Maggie asked when he walked into the kitchen the next morning.

"Maggie, he just woke up. How would he have heard?" Kitty asked. She was unable to tolerate any illogic.

Maggie ignored her and hurried on. "Our aunt is coming."

"The one from New York?" Will asked, and Libby, Kitty, and Maggie looked at him in surprise.

"How did you hear about her?" Maggie asked. "Sometimes I forget she exists. No, I mean Dad's younger sister, Marie. She had a new baby, and she's bringing all the cousins with her."

Anne walked in the door followed by Dobbie, and they groaned in unison when they heard.

"Oh no, not the brat pack," Dobbie said. He sat and Libby poured him a cup of coffee. "My nerves can't take another visit from that bunch. Thanks, Lib."

"When are they coming?" Anne asked. She sat beside Will, and he had to resist the urge to put his arm around her. They hadn't touched since the party at the Henshaw's, but the little they had was like a cruel taste of what he was missing.

"Today," Libby said. She sounded exhausted and frazzled. "Dad forgot to tell me until this morning, and now I have to figure out where they're all going to sleep and figure out menus."

"Make what you were already going to," Dobbie said. "They won't expect anything special, and your food is always good. Don't make it harder on yourself than you need to."

Libby nodded and relaxed visibly.

"Where can we go?" Anne asked Dobbie.

"Too bad the cattle drive is over. We could have used that as an excuse. I suppose we can find something that needs done in the north pasture," Dobbie said.

"Are they really that bad?" Will asked.

Everyone looked at him and nodded in unison.

"Marie is great," Libby said. "She's Dad's opposite, and they drive each other crazy, but her four boys have the combined energy of a flock of newborn lambs. They go in four different directions at once, and they never stop talking or getting into things."

"You know, Ashley, technically you're paid to tutor all the kids in this family," Anne said.

"Nice try, Annie. I don't think four little boys would enjoy doing schoolwork while they're here, but maybe I can think of some fun activities for them. I mean, this is a ranch, and I grew up in a family of three boys."

The rest of the family looked at him with something like hopeful adoration.

"I'm not doing it alone, though. Everyone is going to help," he said.

"If you think you can keep them corralled, then we'll try and help out," Dobbie promised.

Will spent the rest of the morning thinking up activities for the four boys to do. By the time the family arrived by car from Oregon he thought he had everything covered, but then they erupted from their minivan like a whirlwind and he was momentarily caught off guard. They were five, six, seven, and eight, and all their names started with an E. Will didn't try to learn their names because they were moving too fast to pin down.

Marie emerged and unbuckled her newborn baby daughter. She hugged her nieces and Dobbie.

"Is my brother too busy to greet his only little sister?" she asked.

No one knew how to say that her only brother was in the pasture avoiding his little sister, so instead Libby introduced Will.

"Aunt Marie, this is our tutor, Will Ashley. He's from Pittsburgh, and he's here for the summer."

"A city boy?" Marie said delightedly. "Finally Matt did something right by these girls. Maybe you can help give them the education they're lacking." She turned to face the yard. "Boys, carry your bags to the house, and if I have to tell you a second time you won't get any of Libby's desserts." All four of the boys appeared from nowhere and started to carry their bags to the house.

It was lunchtime, so Libby served them some food and they sat quietly for the meal. As soon as their appetites were filled, they started to squirm in their seats, and Will could see the calculating looks on their faces as they plotted what to get into first.

"How are you guys at finding hidden treasure?" Will asked casually.

All four of them perked up and looked at him in interest. "Really good," the oldest one said. "Why?"

"I heard there's something hidden somewhere on the ranch, and I thought you guys might be able to find it. If you're not afraid, that is. It could get sort of dangerous."

"We're not afraid of nothing," the oldest said again.

"Anything," Will corrected automatically. "Okay, I'm going to give you the map, but you have to promise to get help if it gets too scary or dangerous."

The oldest one puckered his little face into a mutinous scowl. "We don't need no help."

"Any," Will said. He retrieved the map he had made and handed it to the oldest boy. The boys huddled together for a while and took off without asking to be excused or cleaning up.

"I suppose I should reprimand them," Marie said. "But the baby gets me up every two hours, and I'm exhausted. This is why people don't have babies when they're forty."

"Go take a nap," Libby said. "I'll watch the baby."

"I'll help," Kitty volunteered.

"Me, too," Maggie chimed in.

Marie smiled and handed the baby to Libby. "She just ate, so she's good for a couple of hours. Thanks, girls, and Will." She turned and headed to her guest room.

Libby sat on the couch with Maggie and Kitty on either side of her. Will stood back to watch. Of course Libby was a natural with babies. She instinctively knew what to do, and she smiled and cuddled and cooed to the baby, who was the tiniest, pinkest human being Will had ever seen. She looked up and noticed his inspection.

"Do you want to hold her, Will?"

"Sure," he said. He sat in the loveseat, and she placed the baby in his arms. He had never held a baby before, but it wasn't so hard. Libby admonished him to support her neck and head. The baby, whose name was Eloise, was asleep. So as long as her status didn't change, Will would be all right. He sensed, rather than saw, that Anne had entered the room and looked up to see her watching him with an inscrutable expression.

"The boys ran into the woods," she said.

"I sent them there looking for treasure. They'll be out as soon as they find their next map," he said. "Want to hold the baby?"

She shook her head. "The last baby I held was Maggie."

"Then you're overdue. Come on, this is the first baby I've ever held. If I can do it you can." She looked like she was going to refuse again. "Chicken," he added, and it worked.

She narrowed her eyes at him, took off her leather work gloves, and held out her arms. Her sisters watched in amazement as Will patted the loveseat beside him, and then placed the baby in Anne's arms when she sat. At first she held herself stiffly and uncomfortably. But when she became used to the feel of the baby in her arms she relaxed slightly and leaned against Will. It was the most natural thing in the world to put his arm around her so he could lean close and peer at the baby. They spent a few minutes talking to the newborn and studying her tiny hands. When they looked up Libby, Kitty, and even Maggie were staring at them in silence.

"What?" Anne asked, and her tone was defensive.

"Nothing," Maggie answered quickly. "You look kind of like a family together. It's strange."

Anne stood and shoved the baby back at Libby. "I have work to do." She stormed out of the house without a backwards glance.

A moment after she left, the boys burst into the room.

"We found the treasure," the oldest one said triumphantly. He held up a bag of candy. They were so loud Will was afraid they would wake Marie, so he herded them outside.

"I have a new game for you, if you're not too tired from your treasure hunt," he said.

"We're not tired at all," the youngest one said. He tried to stifle a yawn, and his brother jabbed him in the ribs.

"How would you guys like to be the police and hunt down some bad guys who escaped into the woods?" Will asked.

Their eyes shone with excitement and a little bit of fear.

"Not real bad guys," Will explained. "Just me and Anne pretending to be bad guys."

"Anne won't play," the oldest one said. "She never plays with us. She's always too busy."

"She'll play this time," Will assured them. "Let's go into the barn to ask her." He hadn't seen her go into the barn, but he had learned it was her place of solace. He had no doubt he would find her there, and he was correct. "There's my partner in crime," he said, and she whirled to look at him. Her angry features softened when she took in the boys' faces behind him.

"What are you lot up to?" she asked.

"We're playing a game, and you have to help us," Will said.

She started to say she was busy, but he interrupted her.

"This one," he put his hand on the oldest boy's head, "says you're always too busy to play with them, but I told them that's not true. I said you would definitely play with us this time."

She suppressed a grimace and tried to smile. "Sure. What are we playing?"

"You and I are the bad guys. We have to hide in the woods, and these police men are going to find us."

"All right," Anne agreed. She set down whatever it was she had been working on and took off her leather work gloves again.

Will took off his watch and set the alarm for eight minutes. "When this beeps you have to come find us. No cheating, because it's going to take us a while to find a good hiding place. And you four have to stick together in the woods, do you promise?"

"We promise," the oldest one answered. He was apparently the spokesperson for his little brothers. "And we don't cheat."

"Good," Will answered. He handed him the watch, patted him on the head, took Anne's hand and tugged her toward the woods.

"You surprise me, Ashley," Anne said.

"On a daily basis, I would guess. Why today?"

"I would have supposed you thought playing in the woods was too dangerous for little boys," she said.

Will swallowed down his irritation with difficulty. "Annie, let's get something straight once and for all. I may not be the type of man you're used to, but I'm still a man. I grew up with two older brothers, and it's a wonder I survived some of the crazy stunts we pulled. I firmly believe kids today are too coddled and need more freedom and space to be kids. The ranch is a perfect place for that." He paused. He was used to Pittsburgh, and he hadn't accounted for the wilderness of Montana. "They won't get attacked by wolves or grizzlies, will they?"

"Depends on how far in they go," she said seriously. She smiled when he turned to look at her in alarm. "Don't worry; they stay close to the mountain during the day. As long as the boys stay together I'm sure they'll be fine. The four of them together might be tougher and wilier than a pack of wolves anyway. Where are we going?"

"You tell me. That's why I brought you. I don't know anything about these woods. I figure you know all the good hiding places."

"You figure correctly." She took over the lead and headed toward a dense grove of tall trees. When they reached it close up he noticed an old dead tree hollowed out on the inside. There would only be enough room for both of them if they squeezed tightly together.

"Are you afraid of bugs and spiders?" she asked.

"Not today," he answered, pushing her into the opening and squeezing in behind her.

"I found this spot for you," she said. "I was going to go hide over there." She couldn't point because there wasn't room.

"We should stick together," he said. "To ward off the wolves and grizzlies."

She laughed and it was the first time he heard her giggle. "Tell me about some of your adventures with your brothers. What kinds of trouble did you get into in the city?"

"We weren't always in the city. My grandparents live in Maryland in the suburbs, and we visited them every summer. We used to sharpen sticks to a point and hunt for snakes. When we didn't find any, we threw them at each other in a jousting competition. We made miniature buildings and blew them up with firecrackers. We had rotten tomato fights; Mom loved those. We bundled each other up in blankets and dragged each other down the stairs. We had wrestling tournaments and jumped over things with our bikes. We had contests to see who could do the biggest wheelie."

"Sounds cutthroat," she said.

"It was. Everything was a competition. It still is. I'm always last because I'm the youngest. Although my brothers have toned down since they became serious about their girlfriends."

"Neither is married?" she asked.

He shook his head.

"How old are they?"

"Twenty-three and twenty-five."

"Around here that's sort of old not to be married. I guess we get married young because we're family oriented, and there isn't much else to do."

"When do you think you and Dobbie will get married?" he asked.

"Oh." Her smile fled, and he chastised himself for bringing up the topic. "In the near future, I guess. Maybe in a couple of years."

He put his hands on her waist. "Annie, you can't marry him. You don't love him."

"Yes, I do," she said stubbornly.

"Fine, maybe you love him, but you're not in love with him."

"And you're such an expert because you've been in love with your many, many girlfriends," she said crossly. She would have moved out of his embrace, but there was nowhere to go.

"I've never been in love before." *Before now*, he wanted to add, but didn't.

"Then what makes you certain?" Her tone was more pleading than accusatory now.

"Maybe it's not certainty. Maybe it's wishful thinking. I don't want you to marry Dobbie."

"What business is it of yours?" she asked softly. "Your time here is almost up. You'll go away and never come back. I'll be left with…" She almost said, *With nothing*. "With memories. Why should I ruin my life, and his, for a phantom?"

"It doesn't have to be like that," he said.

"Then how could it be, Will? I'm committed to the ranch for life. You live thousands of miles away."

"I graduate in two years. I'll come back here. I love the ranch."

"I know you do," she said in the softest, gentlest tone he had ever heard her use. "But what would you do? Kitty and Maggie won't need a tutor by then. You don't know anything about ranching. Would you really be content to sit back and let me support you?"

"No, of course not, but there has to be some solution to this."

"There is. You go back to where you came from, and my life will go on the way it was before."

He studied her in silence. "Is that what you want, Annie? Is that truly what you want?"

She swallowed hard. "I…It doesn't matter what I want."

"It matters to me," he said.

She let out a frustrated breath. "Will, why can't you leave me be? Why do you keep trying to pick at my weak spots? My life is the way it is, and there's no changing it. Enjoy your time here, and then move on."

"You're the best part of my time here, and you're not happy."

"Who says?"

"Your face. Your tears. I can't stop trying to find out what's going on in your head. Tell me and let me help you."

"You can't help me. You can't change anything. No one can." Her eyes filled with tears, but she refused to let them overflow. He tipped her face up and kissed her closed and brimming eyelids. She kept her eyes closed as he moved slowly down to her mouth. Their lips barely touched when they heard the telltale rustle of the four boys nearby. Anne opened her eyes and looked at Will. If she kept silent the boys would go away, and they could finish what they started, but what was the point? Will read her mind and shook his head.

"I hope the boys don't find us," she said as loudly as she could without shouting, and less than a minute later all four boys were pulling them out of the tree and pretending to handcuff them before leading them back to the house.

It was suppertime when they returned. The boys were starting to droop, but food revived them, and they looked at Will for direction.

"I think there might be some money in the barn," he said. He pulled out a metal detector and led them to a hay mound in the barn where he had scattered loose change, along with some washers and nails. The boys spent the next couple of hours until bedtime looking for money in the hay, and then they fell into an exhausted sleep.

"Have you ever considered being a nanny, Will?" Marie asked. "I'll pay you double whatever Matt is."

"The boy has more ambition than to play nursemaid to your brood, Marie," Matt said.

"I was teasing him, Matt. Looks like your sense of humor is still missing," Marie said.

"They're like this whenever they get together," Anne whispered to Will.

Will was fascinated by the dynamic. Even the spirited Anne

deferred to her father. Marie was the first person he encountered who seemed wholly unconcerned by his intimidating presence and foreboding silences.

"My sense of humor is fine," Matt said. "Strange how it takes a hike whenever you show up, little sister." He reached over and ruffled her hair, and she smacked his hand away.

"Quit. I'm not five anymore," she said.

"As if I need that reminder," Matt said, eyeing the seats her children had vacated. "Please tell me you're done."

"I thought I was done before, but I'm glad I wasn't. I finally got my girl."

"Dad wanted all boys," Anne whispered. "Aunt Marie wanted all girls. It's been a sore spot between them for years."

Will wondered if it would bother Matt that Marie finally had her girl while Matt was still without a boy, but then the older man stood and clapped Dobbie on the shoulder, and Will thought maybe he had found a son, after all. Dobbie certainly seemed to love and respect Matt as much as he would his own father.

CHAPTER 17

One of the first things Will learned about the ranch was that everyone rose early. He was a morning person, but even he had to adjust his schedule and rise earlier than usual. This morning, however, he was awakened earlier than usual by four little boys who ran into his room and jumped on his bed.

"What are we going to do today, Uncle Will?" the youngest one said as he jumped up and down on the mattress.

"He's not your uncle," the oldest one said.

"Then what is he?" one of the middle ones asked.

"He's," the oldest one started again and broke off, studying Will. "What are you?"

"I'm a friend of your cousins', so I guess that makes us sort of like cousins, too."

"See, I told you he was our uncle," the youngest one said.

"A cousin isn't the same as an uncle, dummy," the oldest one said. He turned to Will again. "Is it?"

"No, but it's not nice to call your brother a dummy. Matt is your uncle, and his kids are your cousins."

"Is Dobbie our cousin, too?" one of the middle ones asked.

"Sort of," Will answered. It was too early in the morning to get into the complicated family dynamic. "Why don't you guys go get dressed, and then we'll meet downstairs for breakfast.

"Are we going to do lots of fun stuff again today?" the littlest one asked.

"Maybe, if you're very good, and eat all your breakfast, and brush your teeth," Will said.

They shot out of the room without further protest and he heard them loudly asking their mother for their clothes.

He also dressed hurriedly and scrambled downstairs. He wanted to catch Anne before she left the house for the day.

"I need your help," he said as she was leaving.

She paused and turned back to him with a wary, suspicious expression. "Doing what?"

"I thought we would take the boys on a nature ride today," he said.

"We don't have enough horses for them," Anne said.

"The two littlest ones can share with us, and the two oldest can share one of their own. That way we'll only need one extra horse for them," he said. He knew she would try to get out of it by using the horses as an excuse.

She paused and tried to think up another reason not to go. When she couldn't come up with one, she sighed reluctantly. "You know, I do work here for a living."

"And you haven't had a day off in six years. You're overdue."

She rolled her eyes, but she smiled. Her smile increased as she watched Will with the boys. He wouldn't tell them what they were doing for the day, and the suspense kept them on the edges of their seats.

"We're really going to ride horses?" the oldest one, Eli, asked after breakfast as they walked to the barn. Anne felt bad. They had been visiting every year since their birth, but they had never ridden the horses. There were so many of them, and they were so rowdy no one ever wanted to take the time or energy to ride with them.

"You're going to have to be real cowboys," Will said. "It's not easy to sit in the saddle all day and control horses that are bigger than you. Do you think you can do it?"

The four boys nodded solemnly, and listened with rapt attention as Anne explained how to saddle the horses. She and Will helped the boys mount, and she gave Eli a lesson in how to control his horse. She held Eric, the youngest, and Will held Elliot, the next youngest, and then they set off.

She smiled happily as the boys exclaimed over everything they saw. Hearing their excited chatter made her remember her fascination with the ranch when she was a young girl. She couldn't get enough of it, unlike now when she felt chained to it. When had ranch life become a drudge to her, instead of an enjoyment? Did everyone feel this way about their lives, or was it only because her choice had been taken from her that resentment was building inside? She glanced at Will. Was he the reason for her growing dissatisfaction? Always before she thought her life was pegged out, but now she was starting to wonder. What if she didn't marry Dobbie? What if she left the ranch?

She shuddered with a repressed shiver and tried to push away her thoughts. She hated to admit it, even to herself, but she was afraid. If she left the ranch where would she go? What would she do? There was no sense pondering the inevitable. She would marry Dobbie, and they would both live and work here forever.

She gave one more wistful glance at Will. What would it be like to be married to Will? As much as she had tried to push them away, his words to her from his first day kept swimming in her head. What would it be like to have a real partner in her husband? Someone who took care of her when she was sick and helped her raise kids? She tried to picture Dobbie holding her hair back from the toilet when she was ill and almost laughed. Dobbie might spare her from working that day, but that would be the extent of his sympathy. Of course, maybe it was because she had never given him the chance to comfort her. She didn't allow herself to be soft or vulnerable around him, only Will. What was it that enabled him to sidestep her defenses and pinpoint her weak spots? Everyone else thought she was as cold and hard as ice. Only Will saw beyond the façade to the scared and hurt girl she truly was.

She didn't like it that she was transparent to him. She didn't like how much she had come to depend on him in such a short time. Now when something happened to her, either good or bad, her first thought was to tell Will about it. What would it be like after he left? Would she ever get over it, over him?

"You're quiet," Will said.

"I'm always quiet," she said. Only he had the ability to draw her out and get her to open up.

"Except when you're yelling or throwing something at me," he returned. "Deep thoughts?"

She didn't feel like sharing what was on her heart or mind, so she kept silent.

"What's that?" Eli asked. Will and Anne looked where he was pointing and saw a small, crudely constructed lean to.

"I've never seen it before, but I don't come this way often," Anne said.

"Let's check it out," Will said. He dismounted and helped the boys off their horses.

"Maybe robbers made it," Elliot said.

Anne smiled. More likely Maggie had made it. She lived her life in these woods, most of the time with Mathew Henshaw. Her theory was proved correct when Eli pointed to some initials carved into the wood.

"Who are M.H. and M.C?" he asked.

"Maggie and her friend," Anne replied.

"Maybe you guys could gather some moss to cover the floor inside," Will said.

"Okay," they agreed and scuttled away to look for moss.

Will pulled out his pocket knife and began to carve alongside Maggie's initials.

"What are you doing?" Anne asked.

He ignored her and continued carving. When he finished, he stood back and put his arm around her while they surveyed his handiwork together.

"W.A. and A.C. 4Ever," she read out loud.

"Wishful thinking," he said. "Let's pretend this secret hideout is enchanted, and by carving our initials we're making a wish."

"You're fanciful, Ashley," she said, but her tone wasn't disdainful; it was wistful.

The boys started to return with moss. They piled it in the center of the fort's floor and Anne spread it out. Will gathered wildflowers and set them outside the entrance. A soft, gentle rain shower began so the six of them squeezed into the tiny building. Anne started to tell them stories she had learned over the years from the cowhands, and after a while, all four of the little ones were curled up asleep. Will reached over, took her hand, and wove their fingers together. They sat in silence, but it was a cozy silence while the rain softly pattered outside and the boys breathed deeply. For Anne it was one of the best days of her entire life, and Will was busy thinking the same thing.

When they returned to the house, the boys excitedly filled their mother in on their day.

"And Will carved something into the fort," Elliot said. "But I never saw what it was. We fell asleep, but Anne and Will didn't. They must have been tired, though, because they had to hold hands to stay awake."

Will was glad they were alone with Marie. Still, Anne beat a hasty retreat to the barn, and he wanted to follow her when Marie turned to study him with speculation and calculated interest.

Later that night, as he sat on the porch playing a game with the boys, he overheard a discussion between Marie and Matt. He tried to think of a way to avoid eavesdropping, but then his curiosity got the better of him, and he listened unabashedly.

"You're doing wrong by them, Matt," Marie said.

"It's none of your business, Marie," Matt replied.

"It is. They're my nieces, and I have an interest in their futures. Their mother wouldn't want them living like this, and you know it."

"Like what?" he asked defensively.

"Isolated from the outside world and working like draft horses," she said.

"It's no different from how you grew up, and you turned out all right," he said.

"And I moved as far away as I could, as quickly as I could. I still wake up in a cold sweat every calving season, thinking about all the work I had to do to help Mom and Dad."

"I can't help the way it is, Marie. Claire isn't here to help, and she knew what she was getting into when she married me. She knew the girls would be isolated and have to work hard," he said.

"Forever?" Marie asked.

"What are you talking about?" Matt asked with barely controlled anger.

"You seem to have these girls under the impression they're bond-servants who can never leave," Marie said.

"That's ridiculous," Matt said.

"Is it?"

"They can go anywhere and do anything. They happen to love it here."

"Do they?"

"Stop answering a question with a question, little sister. You know I hate that. Spit out whatever you're trying to say and stop beating around the bush," Matt said.

"I'm not saying, I'm asking. If when the time comes the girls want to leave, will you let them go freely and with no cajoling or guilt?"

"Yes," he said.

"You promise?"

"I don't have to promise," he said. "I already said, 'yes.' I've never gone back on my word. I knew if I didn't have sons, I might some day lose the girls to other pursuits. It would be difficult without their help, but I would manage."

"I'm glad to hear that, Matt," Marie said sincerely. They moved on to other topics, but Will tuned them out. He thought maybe he had heard the best news of his life, but didn't yet know what to do with it.

CHAPTER 18

*M*arie and her children went home the next day, and a few days later it was Libby's birthday. When Will found out she was going to make her own cake, he vetoed that idea and volunteered himself and Anne to bake for her.

Dobbie laughed out loud. "Something tells me you can probably cook, but my little Anne should never be allowed in the kitchen. Thank goodness we have Libby, or we would all starve."

Anne put her hands on her hips. "Libby won't always be here, you know. I should probably learn at some point."

He frowned, as if he had never considered a future without Libby.

Will frowned, too. "I don't know how to cook, but it can't be that difficult, can it?"

At that Libby laughed uproariously, and pressed her hand over her mouth when Will and Anne gave her a look.

Anne left the cake selection up to Will, and he chose a cheesecake. He called his mother for a recipe and had to listen to *her* laugh uproariously when he told her he would be the one baking it.

"Honey, cheesecakes require finesse. Why don't you use a boxed cake mix?" she suggested.

"Because there aren't any in the house. Libby makes all her cakes from scratch. She's never had cheesecake before, and I want to do something nice for her."

His mother sighed. "All right, I'll give you the recipe, but you're going to need to do it exactly as I say, step by step."

By the end of the phone call he almost changed his mind about making the cheesecake. It did sound daunting, but he also wanted Libby's sixteenth birthday to be special, so he dove in with Anne as his assistant.

"Okay, first we have to make a graham cracker crust," he said.

"I don't think we have graham crackers," Anne said. "I haven't seen them in the house since Maggie was a baby."

"Oh," Will said, disappointed. It wasn't as if they could run to the store to buy some when the nearest store was over an hour away. He picked up the phone and called his mother again.

"No graham crackers," he said without preamble.

She stifled her laughter. "Make a shortbread crust. That's what the fancy places in New York do." She gave him the recipe for a shortbread crust and disconnected.

Will and Anne studied the recipe and then set out butter and flour. It looked easy enough, but twenty minutes later he called his mother again.

"It's a bunch of crumbles," he said.

"That's what it's supposed to look like," she assured him. "Use the palm of your hand to mash it into the pan, and it will come together."

He hung up, tried it, and learned she was correct.

"That looks good," Anne said. "We might actually be able to pull this off."

"You doubted us?" he said.

"I'm keeping track of how many times you call your mother," she said.

While the crust was baking, they started on the cheesecake. "I can't believe you don't have graham crackers, but you have eight packages of cream cheese in this house," Will said.

"Libby keeps it on hand for some casserole she makes for Dobbie. He loves it."

She said it nonchalantly. Will didn't understand her. "It doesn't bother you they're close?"

"They're not close. They can barely stand each other."

"Annie," he started and then stopped. If she learned the truth, it might hurt her.

Her big eyes hovered on his face as she waited for him to speak. "What?"

She was beautiful, he thought. So special, so unique, so everything. *I love you*, he wanted to say. Instead he said, "Thanks for doing this with me."

She smiled. "It's fun, more fun than I thought it would be. Maybe there's something to this cooking thing. Maybe I should get Libby to teach me."

"When would you have the time? You work harder than anyone I've ever seen."

"I work a normal amount," she said. "You're entrenched in your soft, eastern ways."

"You have me there," he agreed. "I've never been any place where livelihood is attached to land and animals. The people in my world use their brains and not their hands for a living. It seems ironic to me now that I have to go to the gym to stay in shape when everyone here does it by working their normal job." Besides falling in love with Anne, he had fallen in love with the ranch. Everything back home would feel backwards now, he was sure.

She opened the cream cheese packages, and he dumped them into the stand mixer and turned it on. Anne measured the sugar and sour cream, and he added those, too.

"See what a good team we make, Annie?" he asked.

She smiled. "In the kitchen."

"But it doesn't have to end there," he said. She smiled, but didn't respond.

"What do you want to do?" he tried again.

"Finish this cake and have it be edible," she replied

"No, I mean, what do you want to do with your life?" he asked.

"So many questions, Ashley. What has you in such a deep mood?"

He didn't want to put himself out any more today if she wasn't willing to reciprocate. They worked in silence for a while until they poured the cake in the pan, and then they sat at the kitchen table to wait. They were alone in the house. Will reached over and took her hand.

"What did you get Libby for her birthday?" she asked.

"How do you know I got her anything?" he asked.

"You're too thoughtful not to get her anything," she said.

He smiled. "I got her dishtowels."

"That seems like an impersonal gift for how close you guys are."

He had trouble not rolling his eyes. She was clearly jealous of his relationship with Libby but the fact her boyfriend of four years was most likely in love with her seemed to escape her notice.

"Why are you rolling your eyes at me, Ashley?" she asked peevishly.

"Libby and I are friends, as you know," he said.

"You're a lot alike," she said.

"So are you and Dobbie."

"Yes, and we're dating," she pointed out.

"Are you, really? When is the last time you guys made out?"

"I...We," she stopped and blinked at him. "That's none of your business."

"That's what I thought."

She snatched her hand out of his grasp and stood to check the cake. "How do you know when this thing is done?"

"I don't know," he said. He grabbed the phone, called his mother, and asked her. When he hung up Anne was giving him a wistful look. "You miss your mom."

She nodded, and turned away to hide her tears. She quickly swiped her eyes. "Why do you always make me cry, Ashley?"

"I don't make you cry, Annie. I let you cry." He jiggled the cake to make sure it looked done. It did, so he removed it and set it on the counter.

"Stop letting me," she demanded. "I can't keep doing this, Will. I want to survive. I don't want to feel anything."

"You're not surviving if you're not feeling," he said.

"I've been doing it for six years," she said.

"Surviving isn't really living. I don't want to see you pretending to be some closed off shell when I know you're so much more," he said.

She thought that over. Why was he able to see through her defenses when no one else could? She was exhausted from trying to figure it out.

"I need to wrap Libby's present before tonight," she said, excusing herself before he could stop her.

He watched her go with narrowed, concerned eyes. The summer was slipping away, and in some ways he thought they were no closer to a solution than when it began.

CHAPTER 19

After so many emergency calls to his mother during the cake debacle, Will knew better than to attempt to cook supper. Libby made her own birthday supper, but she didn't seem to mind. She kept darting pleased, excited glances at her cake and he knew they did the right thing by making it for her. She blushed prettily when they sang to her, and waited excitedly while everyone retrieved her presents.

She opened Will's first and exclaimed over her dishtowels.

"Thanks, Will, they're so pretty. I'm going to hang them for decoration." She stood and gave him a hug.

"Happy birthday, Libby," he said. Briefly he imagined giving any other girl dishtowels for her sixteenth birthday and almost laughed at the reception he would get, but Libby wasn't like other girls, and she seemed truly delighted by the gift.

When she opened Dobbie's gift she gasped. Her eyes filled with tears.

"It's so pretty," she whispered. She smiled at him, and he returned it, but they made no move to hug. Will wondered if they ever had. Maybe if they did someday, things would explode between them, and they wouldn't be able to deny their attraction for each other anymore.

His mind ran on a tangent as he pictured ways to push them into a hug.

Maggie and Kitty volunteered to clean the kitchen, giving Libby the night off. Anne went to the barn while Libby and Dobbie went into the living room. Will picked up the mug he had bought and followed Anne to the barn.

She was sitting on a pile of fresh hay in one of the horse stalls. He sat beside her. "What's wrong?" he asked.

"Nothing," she said.

"Don't pretend with me."

"Thinking."

"You're going to make me drag it out of you, aren't you?"

She smiled. "About you, and me, and us, Dobbie, the ranch, the future, and life in general."

"That's a lot to think about," he said. Maybe if he treaded lightly, she would tell him what she wanted to do with her life. He sensed it wasn't the ranch, but he knew she felt disloyal admitting it. When she didn't respond, he continued. "Annie, you have given the past six years of your childhood to this ranch and your family. You're only eighteen. You have the right to a life for yourself. Some day your sisters are going to be gone, and so will your dad. What will be left for you?"

"The ranch," she said.

"Does the ranch mean so much to you that you are willing to give up your happiness for it?"

"It's not about my happiness, Ashley. It's about my duty." Anger was creeping into her tone.

"You've done your duty," he said, and he was getting angry, too. No one had ever been able to get under his skin like she did.

"You don't know that. You know nothing about duty and sacrifice."

"And you know more than you should. You're an eighteen year old girl, and you act like a middle aged man." He reached behind him and handed her the mug he had bought her. "Here." He thrust it toward her.

She frowned as she took it out of the bag and unwrapped it. "It's not my birthday," she said softly.

"It doesn't have to be your birthday for me to get you a gift. I bought it because it's pretty and it reminds me of you, and you need something special in your life. Something that's all your own." He was still angry, but he didn't know why. Maybe he was frustrated with the impossible situation, or maybe he was frustrated by her.

Her gaze was wistful, almost hungry when it fastened on the mug. "It's so pretty." She circled the rim with her index finger. Then her face turned hard, and her features closed up. She shoved the mug back at him. "I can't keep this."

"Yes, you can," he said.

"No, I can't," she argued.

He moved out of her reach and then stood and turned his back to her. Thunder rolled outside, and lightning cracked. The sound almost masked her rustling movement, but not quite. When she pounced he was ready for her. He turned and caught her, but her weight made him stumble backwards against the side of the pen.

"Why are you doing this?" he asked. "Do you really want to do this again, Anne? Haven't I proved to you enough that you can't beat me?"

In answer she started to try and fight him. He couldn't do this again. He wouldn't wrestle with her so she could try and convince herself he wasn't getting to her, that she could beat him. Instead of fighting her, he did the only thing he could think of. He kissed her.

Shock made her stop fighting him, and then something else made her twine her fingers in his hair and respond to his kiss. Outside the rain started to pour. When they realized they were isolated by the storm they sank to a sitting position and continued kissing. As the kiss started to wind down, she started to cry. The kiss finally ended and he rested his forehead on hers.

"I cheated," she whispered.

"I'm sorry," he said sincerely. He never meant to cause her to cheat on her boyfriend.

"What am I going to do, Will?" she asked brokenly.

"Listen to your heart for once, Annie," he said softly. He gathered her close and she pressed her cheek to his chest.

"My heart is telling me to do something impossible," she said.

"What? What do you want? Tell me, and I'll make it happen, Anne, I promise I will."

She smiled against his chest, but didn't reply. They stayed that way, huddled together on the hay but not speaking, until the storm passed.

"Come to the north pasture with me," she said. "Some more calves were killed, and I need to look for that wolf or coyote. Plus, I don't want to go inside and face him."

He knew she meant Dobbie. "You can't run away forever."

"It shouldn't have happened. It was a blip, and there's no need for it to ruin everything he and I have." She spoke as she saddled their horses. She took her gun from the locked cabinet in the corner of the barn and slung it over her shoulder.

"Maybe it shouldn't have happened while you two are still together, but it should have happened. It wasn't a blip, and you and he don't have much to ruin. Break up with him, Anne."

"For what? A shadow? A mist?"

"Is that all I am to you?" He swung up onto Maggie's pony.

"Not while you're here, but you'll be gone soon."

"It doesn't have to end."

She nodded. "We live in two different worlds, and when you return to yours you're going to realize it."

He let out a frustrated breath. Talking to her was like beating his head on a rock, only he had better success of making a dent in the rock. Like he did every time they reached an impasse he changed the subject.

"Isn't hunting wolves illegal?" he asked.

"Not if you catch one in the act of hurting or killing livestock."

"Would you really kill one? They're endangered and majestic."

"And taking money from our pockets. If I don't do it, Dad or Dobbie will." She frowned at him because he was frowning at her. "None of us wants to. It's not like we wake up in the morning hoping for the chance to kill a wolf. But they're costing us money, and, as you pointed out, our livelihood is dependent on the cattle they're killing."

"I suppose," he said. He hoped she wouldn't find anything. He didn't think he had the stomach for watching a wolf get shot down.

They rode in silence for a while.

"What happens now?" he asked. "With us."

"There is no 'us.' We go back to the way it was before."

"You mean where I pursue you, and you try to beat me up?" he asked.

She smiled. "Yes. Exactly like that."

"You're not going to tell Dobbie about it?"

"Do you want to die? If I tell him, his anger won't be spent on *me*," she said.

"I can handle him," Will said with more bravado than he felt. He might be able to handle himself in a street fight back home, but Dobbie was accustomed to working with giant, bucking bulls for a living. He didn't like his chances, but he couldn't allow Anne to think he was weak or afraid.

"I don't want to hurt Dobbie. Telling him is one sure way to do that. Let's make sure it doesn't happen again."

"Too bad. It was pretty great."

She tried to look indifferent, but gave up and grinned. "It really was."

They smiled until they reached the north pasture and heard a calf bellowing. In one swift, deft movement, Anne took her gun off her shoulder, aimed, and shot at something Will still couldn't see. His heart sank as he pictured a wolf.

When they reached it Anne kept her gun trained on the animal as she dismounted, but it was dead.

"You can relax, Ashley, it's a coyote. They're a dime a dozen." She checked the calf, sighed, and raised her gun to its head. "Now's the time to look away," she said. She glanced at him to see if he looked away. He didn't, and watched as she shot the injured cow in the head to relieve its misery.

Will had never seen anything die before except for a goldfish he'd had when he was four, and then he had cried for an entire day. To watch two animals be killed within the space of two minutes was disconcerting to him. He understood the necessity in the situation. Now that the coyote realized he could take down calves, there would be no stopping him, and they couldn't afford to lose calves that would some day be large and profitable cows. Killing the cow had been a mercy with its throat ripped open the way it was. Still, he hated to watch it. Despite what Anne thought or said, he was a man with a man's sensibilities. Even though he didn't enjoy death, he could tolerate it without squeamishness or hysteria, but she was a girl. How had she become so calloused that she could drop two mammals without batting an eyelash?

"Why are you looking at me like that?" she asked defensively. "I had to do it."

"I know you did," he said gently.

His gentleness bothered her more than his disdain would have. "Don't," she said, and her voice cracked. She turned away from him. He went forward, took the gun from her hands, laid it on the ground, and turned her to face him. He cupped her face in his hands.

"You had to do it," he said gently.

"I hate it," she whispered. "I hate it all." She could no longer hold back her tears. They came out in a torrent, and she buried her face in his shirt.

Will wanted to kiss her again, but he refrained. She had admitted to him she hated her life, and she had no idea what a big step that was. Now if he could only figure out how to get her to admit what she did want, he could set about making it happen. There had to be a way to make her happy. He wouldn't rest until he figured out what it was.

CHAPTER 20

"Ican't believe you have never been to the fair."

"Never," Will said. He, Maggie, and Anne were in the family pickup truck and driving to the first day of the fair. Maggie was showing chickens and a turkey, and they were riding in cages in the back of the truck. Maggie couldn't stop exclaiming over what she saw as Will's lack of culture.

"Don't you have fairs in Pittsburgh?" she asked.

"It's not really a city type of thing to do," he said. "What would we show, pigeons?" She didn't get the joke, but Anne did and laughed. "My only experience with a fair is watching 'Charlotte's Web.'"

"I can assure you there will be no singing rats or writing spiders."

"That you know of," he said cryptically, and Maggie laughed.

The drive to the fair was long, and Maggie spent it telling Will all the wonders he was about to see.

"And there are animals, and food, and games, and rides, and kids from all over the county. Anne and Dobbie used to stay there, but I'm not allowed." Her lip stuck out in the closest thing to a pout he had ever seen from her.

"Dobbie and I showed cows," Anne soothed. "You don't need to stay with your poultry. Checking them every day will be fine." Some kids did stay with their poultry, but none of the Chapmans would allow Maggie to do so. She was naïve and innocent, and they all protected her.

"Mathew is staying," Maggie said.

"Even more reason for you not to stay," Anne said.

"Why?" Maggie asked, and Will smiled at the innocence in her tone. She hadn't yet discovered boys, and had no idea Mathew Henshaw had a huge crush on her.

"Never mind," Anne said tiredly. She had no desire to explain to her sister why boys and girls shouldn't spend copious amounts of time together. She glanced at Will, and they smiled over Maggie's head. Since Libby's birthday the previous week things had been warm between them, with no repeat of their kiss. Anne felt guilty whenever she saw Dobbie, so she had been avoiding him for days. He didn't seem to notice, which made her feel both relieved and sad.

They finally arrived at the fair, and Maggie started to dart away, but Anne called her back.

"Do I have to stay with you all day?" Maggie asked.

"At least until we find Mathew," Anne said. She didn't want her sister to stay overnight at the fair with him, but he was two years older, more world-wise, and extremely protective of Maggie. He would never let anything happen to her. They didn't have to wait long to meet up with him because, a few minutes after their arrival, he found them.

"Meet us back here at nine, and don't follow strangers, and don't spend all your money on the carnie games," Anne said, but she was looking at Mathew as she spoke because Maggie was already glancing around in anticipation.

Mathew nodded and smiled. "She'll be fine, Anne. Come on, Mags, let's go set up your chickens." He carried the turkey and one chicken while Maggie carried the other chicken, and they set off.

Anne and Will watched them go.

"He seems like a nice kid," Will said.

Anne nodded. "He is. All the Henshaws are nice."

"Why did you and Marcus never get together?"

"I was always with Dobbie. Marcus was sort of our rival, and he always preferred Libby. I outgrew the rivalry, but Dobbie never did." She shook her head. "Men."

"Don't you find it strange Dobbie doesn't hate me?" he asked.

"Yes, it is strange. He's never asked about you and me. He didn't object to us spending the day together today. I guess he trusts me."

"Or he's not in love with you," Will said.

"I don't know," she said, and her frown deepened. She had been chipper, but her mood turned melancholy.

"I didn't mean to upset you," he said.

"After you leave, I expected things to go back to the way they were before you came, but I'm not sure that's possible now. I cheated on Dobbie, I feel horrible, and as you pointed out, we don't exactly have the world's most passionate relationship, but we do have a lot of years and a lot of memories together." She looked around the fair. "We spent a lot of time together here. We had our first kiss at the fair."

He wanted to take her hand, but there were too many people who knew her here. "I'm sorry I've messed things up for you, but you don't have to go back to the way things were, Annie. We can be together."

She shook her head. "Impossible. Even if we weren't miles away in distance we're miles away in temperament, and our futures will never intersect."

Now it was his turn to frown. "I told you I would move here. I'm willing to do whatever it takes to make us happen. I think your pessimism is due more to fear."

"Maybe so, but it's different for you. You get to run away and leave everything that might keep us apart, I have to stay here and face it head on."

"I'll help you."

"How, Ashley? How are you going to help me face Dobbie and my Dad and tell them their dreams of us uniting are over? You're going to be back in Pittsburgh with all your friends, family, and girlfriends while I'm going to be looking in their faces and seeing the disappointment and hurt in their eyes. I can't do that to them. I won't." He started to speak, but she interrupted him. "Let's shelve this pointless discussion and have a nice day today, all right?"

He reluctantly agreed and followed her around as she led him to different stalls, explaining the exhibits to him. She told him what the judges would look for, especially in the cows, and then selected the one she thought might win. They went through the merchant's building, and she stopped to talk to a few people about their products as they related to the ranch. She said hello to several people who all gave Will a curious glance.

They shared fried food for lunch.

"I love my little sister, but she never makes unhealthy fried food like this. I miss it," Anne said.

"You should come to Pittsburgh," Will said. "It's on every corner. I'll show you a good time."

She smiled and shoved a French fry in his mouth.

In the afternoon they went to a hog calling contest.

"Did you ever do this?" Will asked.

"I'll never tell," Anne replied.

After that they went to the fair queen pageant.

"There's a fair queen," Will said incredulously. "It's a whole new world for me."

"There's also a pork princess, beef princess, and dairy princess," Anne said.

"Wow," he mouthed.

"We must seem so backwards to you, Ashley."

"No you don't," he said.

She eyed the girl wearing a pork princess sash.

"Okay, maybe a little bit, but it's different in a good kind of way. Sometimes in the city you feel out of touch with reality. Everything can be cold, sterile, and dirty. There's a lot of crime, and everything moves at a faster pace. Here people enjoy life. You understand the fragility of life because you're closely tied to the earth. Plus it's the most beautiful place I've ever seen, with the most beautiful people." He winked at her, and then gasped. "Did you just blush?"

She pressed her lips together and looked away without answering.

"You could teach a master's course in avoidance techniques," he said.

"And you could teach one in mindless flattery," she said.

"Maybe so, but it doesn't mean I'm not sincere."

"Oh, geez," she muttered.

They met up with Maggie and Mathew for supper. After supper, a huge crowd began milling toward the large arena for a demolition derby.

"I've seen one of these before," Will said. "They have it in the arena in Pittsburgh, but you have to pay a lot more money."

Maggie and Mathew were lost in their own world. Anne and Will observed them for a while.

"Was it ever like that for you and Dobbie?" he asked.

"I suppose or we wouldn't have started dating. But it's been so long ago I don't remember. Now it's all about the ranch." She turned to study him. "What about you, do you remember your first love?"

He knew he had never been in love with any of the girls he dated. He knew because he was in love with her, and he had never felt this way before. "I remember it distinctly," he said.

Something in his tone must have alerted her to his meaning because she blushed again and faced forward to watch the start of the derby. The show was properly entertaining, with lots of crashes and car parts falling off. Some entrants had cleverly designed cars that allowed them to outwit the competition. The slower, clumsier cars, or "easy losers" as Anne called them, were picked off early. By the end the competition was fierce, and only the skilled drivers or tank-like vehicles survived the many collisions. Finally there were only two competitors left, and they were brothers who were well known by the crowd. Everyone stood to their feet for the final half hour. Eventually the younger brother won, and the audience clapped for a long time.

"What does he win?" Will asked.

"This," Anne said, and clapped louder.

"He went through all that for applause?"

Anne nodded. "There's not much else going on here, and he's won bragging rights for an entire year. What could he really win, a gift certificate for the feed store?"

Will tried to imagine buying a car, modifying it to withstand damage, and spending two hours wrecking it so he could claim victory. He would never do such a thing in Pittsburgh with so many other distractions, but maybe if he lived here, he would find such a hobby interesting. Somehow he doubted it.

Anne must have guessed his thoughts. "Even out here there are some who are more into the country scene than others. Some people lavish attention on their tractors the way others lavish attention on sports cars. Some are into horses. Others, like the Henshaws, are above it all. If you ran into them in the city you probably wouldn't be able to tell they lived in the middle of nowhere."

"If I ran into you in the city I would never guess you live on a ranch," he said.

"Really?" She looked up at him to see if he meant it, and seemed delighted by his answer. Did she want to look like she blended into city life?

"Annie," he started to ask her again what she wanted out of life, but Maggie broke away from Mathew, so he shelved the discussion.

To his surprise Anne tossed him the keys to the truck.

"I don't feel like driving," she explained. He thought her trust in his driving skills was a point in his favor until she continued. "You *can* drive, right?"

"Yes, I can drive. I'm a man. I do manly things on occasion."

She grinned. "That's becoming more believable."

"Be still my heart," he said. "She thinks I'm masculine."

"Let's not push it," Anne replied. "I no longer think of you as a girl. I'm not ready to go farther than that for tonight."

For the first half of the ride home Maggie chattered excitedly about all she had seen and done that day. She sat between them, and then fell silent for the remainder of the drive. When they pulled up the long lane leading to the ranch, Will realized she was asleep. Anne started to wake her, but Will shook his head.

"I'll carry her," he whispered.

Anne gave him a dubious look and started to protest. "She's almost as tall as me," she whispered.

"That's because you're tiny, too," he said. He slid Maggie across the seat and easily picked her up. He enjoyed the surprised look on Anne's face. Where he was from, no one ever questioned his masculinity. It was a new experience to have to prove his manhood to a girl. It both annoyed and amused him to have to do so now.

They reached the porch and the sound of arguing inside the house roused Maggie awake. She looked around in confusion and slid out of Will's grasp. They entered the house together and stopped short at the sight that greeted them.

Dobbie was standing in front of the couch and he was holding Libby upside down by the ankles. One arm was wrapped around her calves, pinning her dress to her legs so it didn't fly over her head. They were so involved in their heated argument they didn't hear Anne, Will, and Maggie enter the room.

"Put me down," Libby yelled.

"No," Dobbie said.

Libby hitched up his jeans and bit his shin, hard.

He yelped in pain, but still laid her down gently, and bent to rub his leg before straightening. They stood toe to toe frowning at each other.

"Libby, you had better go to bed before I do something I regret," he said.

"What? Like hold me upside down? That was not a gentlemanly thing to do."

"Since when have I ever been a gentleman? Besides, I doubt you'll find biting someone on the shin in the 'Ladies' Code of Conduct Manual' you seem to have memorized."

"I wouldn't have had to bite you if you hadn't picked me up," she yelled.

"I wouldn't have picked you up if you hadn't stolen the remote," he yelled.

"I wouldn't have stolen the remote if you didn't insist on flipping through the channels so fast it practically made a strobe light on the screen."

"Go to bed," he said through clenched teeth.

She crossed her arms over her chest. "You can't tell me what to do."

"I just did."

"Doesn't mean I have to listen," she said.

They stared each other down for another minute, and then he picked her up by the waist, threw her over his shoulder, and carried her up the stairs. He brushed by Anne, Will, and Maggie without speaking. They looked at each other and then darted up the stairs behind Libby and Dobbie. Dobbie opened Libby's door and tossed her inside, but before he could stop her, she grabbed his white Stetson and locked the door behind herself.

He banged on the door. "Give that back."

"Not until you learn some manners," she said.

"Woman," he yelled. "Don't make me break down this door."

"Break down the door and I'll throw your hat out the window," she said.

At that point Matt stepped out of his room. "What's the ruckus?"

Dobbie opened his mouth to speak, thought better of it, and then turned and stomped down the stairs and out the door.

Matt stared at the hallway for a minute, shook his head, and went back into his room.

"Goodnight," Maggie said cheerfully and went into her room.

Will double-checked the deserted hallway to make sure he and Anne were alone.

"Looks like Dobbie and Libby started *World War III*," he said.

"Nah," Anne replied. "This is an almost nightly occurrence for them. They'll both be over it by morning, and she'll probably make his favorite breakfast of waffles."

Will nodded and looked down the stairs. "He didn't kiss you goodnight."

Anne followed his gaze with a frown. "True."

"Someone should," Will said. Before she could protest he tipped her face up and gave her a soft, sweet, kiss, and then he went into his room.

The next morning he sat down at the table and smiled when Libby plated a waffle and set it before him.

CHAPTER 21

On Thursday they went to the fair again. Maggie had to be there every day, and the family took turns going with her. Tuesday Dobbie and Kitty went. Wednesday her father escorted her, and on Friday she would be going with the Henshaws. Libby was the only family member who skipped her turn as escort. The garden was starting to reach its peak, and she was busy canning from sunup until sundown on some days.

Mathew Henshaw wouldn't arrive until later that night, so Maggie spent the day with Anne and Will. She walked between them and clasped their hands, and Will had to repress an almost constant smile. She was a different girl, but so sweet and lovable the other kids her age who knew her didn't make fun of her for her girlish ways. Instead they smiled and waved and said hello as if she were a favorite friend. And no wonder, she was kind and friendly to everyone, especially the disenfranchised kids they saw, like the ones who looked like they would be labeled special education, or those who had physical disabilities. She went out of her way to talk to them, and Will noticed Anne watching her with a soft affection, too. Out of all the Chapmans, Maggie came closest to accessing the deepest recesses of Anne's guarded heart, the one Will had glimpsed and knew existed deep down.

After lunch they attended a dog agility competition, and Will realized he hadn't noticed any dogs on the ranch.

"Why don't you guys have a dog?" Will asked.

"We've had lots and lots of dogs," Maggie volunteered. "The coyotes and wolves get them, except one that was killed by a rattlesnake. Anne said we're not allowed to get any more because they're too much trouble to watch after, and too much hassle to replace." She said it matter of factly, and Will watched Anne's face as Maggie spoke. She stared straight ahead and wouldn't look at him, but he knew the truth. The reason she didn't want any more dogs was because it was too painful for her when they died.

"Maybe you could have a dog that lives indoors," he suggested.

Maggie shook her head. "Libby said she has enough to clean up with all of us Chapmans and Dobbie to look after. She doesn't need to add animal mess into the mix."

Will smiled again. It was the same reason his mother had given. Maggie didn't find her situation abnormal now, but how would it affect her when she grew up and realized her oldest sisters functioned as her mother and father? Would she feel appreciation or bitterness? He had a difficult time picturing Maggie being bitter over anything. He hoped nothing would happen to change her sweet, selfless innocence.

Mathew Henshaw arrived before supper and the four of them ate together.

"What's tonight's event?" Will asked. He learned the fair held a different activity each night.

"The dance," Mathew said.

"Oh, no," Maggie exclaimed. "I don't want to spend the whole night dancing. Do you want to go to the cow barn?" she asked Mathew.

"But, I," he paused, looking flustered. It was obvious to Will the boy wanted to spend the entire night dancing with Maggie, but wasn't sure how to bring it about. "Sure," he said at last. Maggie missed the reluctance in his tone and smiled happily.

Will winked at Anne over Mathew's head. She smiled and looked away.

If only *she* could think of an excuse to get out of the dance. Why did she have to choose tonight of all nights to attend the fair again? Why couldn't they have come last night for the tractor pull? She should have remembered they held the dance on Thursdays. She tried to take a deep breath but couldn't. The suffocating feeling was back, and worse than ever before. Will was leaving in two weeks, and he was becoming more a part of her life, not less. Dobbie had finally realized she was avoiding him and called her on it.

"Are you angry with me about something, Anne?" he asked yesterday.

"No," she said shortly, turning her back to him. She was afraid he might be able to read the truth in her eyes.

"Then what's wrong?" he asked irritably. They never talked about feelings together, and she had no idea how to let him in on her inner thoughts and emotions.

"I have a lot on my mind," she said, which was true.

He stared at her in consternation. If she didn't know how to open up to him, he certainly didn't know how to get her to open up. For a few minutes they participated in a silent standoff.

"I looked at rings," he blurted, and that made her turn around and look at him.

"What?"

"I looked at engagement rings." He said it like a challenge and raised his chin a notch.

Her mouth opened slightly.

"I didn't buy one," he continued.

She still didn't know what to say, and her silence angered him further.

"Nothing? You have nothing to say? We've been dating for four years, I told you I've been looking at engagement rings, and you have nothing to say to me."

"I'm not ready to get married yet," she said at last.

He relaxed slightly. Did he look relieved, or was it her imagination? "I'm not either. We're only eighteen. That's why I didn't buy a ring, but someday soon we should probably set a timeline."

She swallowed hard, but she relaxed, too. Setting a timeline someday was much less scary than getting engaged now.

Will took her hand to lead her onto the dance floor, and it jogged her back to the present, but the oppressive feeling of fear remained. She took a surreptitious glance around at the other people near them. Many of them were acquaintances she had known all her life. Did they suspect the chemistry between her and Will? Would they tell her father and Dobbie about the intimate way he was holding her in his arms?

"Relax, Annie, I'm sure everyone thinks we're just friends," he said.

His possession of the uncanny ability to read her mind was disconcerting, to say the least. No one, but no one ever knew what went on inside her because she didn't let them. She had to be tough. She had to make the difficult decisions and do the right thing, always. No matter how she might feel about it. She had to discipline her sisters when, in reality, she wanted to hug them, and comfort them, and dry their tears. She had to listen to her father lecture her on her management decisions regarding the ranch, when really she wanted to hear him chastise her for spending too much money on pretty clothes or staying out too late on a date. She had to date Dobbie, the most reasonable choice for her, when she wanted nothing more than to fling her arms around Will and follow him to the ends of the earth. Most of all, she had to be strong and independent when what she wanted was to be taken care of for once. Specifically, she wanted Will to take care of her. She wanted his tenderness and affection because the rare times she had experienced it, she had soaked it up like a sponge, even though she had pretended to resent it. She couldn't admit it to him, but he had won her over to his way of thinking completely. No longer did she doubt him. He was masculine as well as loving, strong and gentle. The combination didn't repulse her. No, it fascinated and entranced her. How could she ever be content with anyone else when he had become her ideal?

She had to do something, anything, to get away from him before she fell apart completely. If she allowed herself to get any closer to him, she wouldn't survive when he went away.

"I suppose you dance with lots of girls back home," she said curtly.

"Not like this," he said, and smiled at her.

She stifled a sigh. How did he do that? How did he so easily deflect her anger with a comment that made her knees weak?

She was saved from further introspection when the pace of the music picked up and he spun her away from him. For a while the music was loud and fast, cutting out the possibility of conversation. Eventually a slow song came on again, and he pulled her close.

"People are going to talk," she said.

"They would talk more if I held you awkwardly and stiffly away from me. This is normal. Relax, Annie."

"Don't call me that," she said.

He smiled but didn't comment. The knowledge that he knew exactly what she was up to made her even more desperate to get away from him.

"We should check on Maggie," she said. She wrenched out of his grasp and stalked away.

He easily caught up with her. "Aren't you going to try and beat me up?" he asked. "That's what you usually do whenever I start getting too close to you."

"You've been too close to me since you arrived," she said. She picked up her pace, but she was no match for his long legs. He easily outpaced her and paused to wait for her to catch up with him.

"Stop that," she said.

"Stop what?" he asked innocently.

"Stop doing whatever it is you're doing. Stop playing games with me."

"Then stop running from me," he said heatedly.

"No," she said and gasped when he took her hand and roughly tugged her behind him. He pulled her to the deserted side of the equestrian building. They barely stopped before he kissed her. She didn't even think of protesting because she wanted to kiss him as much as he wanted to kiss her.

Let me have this, she thought. *Just let me have this one night of stolen perfection with Will, and I will uncomplainingly return to my dreary existence.*

They kissed for a long time, until the murmur of voices and the shuffling of feet alerted them to the fact the dance was over, and the fair was closing.

"We should find Maggie," she whispered.

Will nodded. She turned to go, but he held her back. "I love you," he said. He touched his palm to her cheek. "I love you so much, Annie." She was glad he didn't wait for a reply. Instead he took her hand and led her away.

She wondered if he could feel her hand shaking in his. Fear rose like bile in the back of her throat. Surely he didn't mean it. He didn't know what he was saying. This couldn't be happening. It was one thing to have a summer flirtation with him, but if he was in love with her he wouldn't let her go. He would persist in pursuing her, and her life as she knew it would come crashing down around her ears. If she were the only one involved, she would celebrate. But she couldn't do that. She had a responsibility to her family, and she had to think of them. One way or another, she had to push him away, and her mind went into overdrive as she tried to figure out how.

CHAPTER 22

*W*ill woke the next morning feeling something like remorse. After their kiss last night, he had been overcome with emotion and blurted out the truth of his feelings to Anne. He should have waited until she was ready to hear them, and now he was paying the piper. Her cool avoidance was worse than her anger.

She deflected his attempts to speak with her by surrounding herself with her family or Dobbie. She wouldn't talk to him directly or even look at him. At first he was angry and hurt. If he was smart he would forget her. He would walk away at the end of this summer without looking back. He would pretend she didn't exist. He would find a normal girl with normal emotions who actually wanted his attention.

Even as he thought it, he dismissed the idea. He didn't want anyone else. He wanted Anne, forever.

For a few days after the fair he let her stew, but when he realized she wasn't coming around and talking to him again, he became desperate. What should he do? What could he do? Scenarios swirled in his head. Maybe he should talk to Matt and tell him the truth of the situation.

Sir, I'm in love with your daughter, he imagined himself saying. *You know, the foreman of your ranch—the one who keeps things running, the one your livelihood depends on. The one who is supposed to complete your dream of having a son by marrying Dobbie. Anyway, I'm probably terrible at ranching, but if you let me marry Anne and live here, I'll try to pull my weight. I'm sure Libby needs a helper in the kitchen.*

He grimaced. Maybe Matt wasn't the way to go. Maybe he should confess everything to Dobbie. The younger man would no doubt demand a duel of some sort, and Will didn't think he would concede to a battle of the wits.

I'll play you Trivial Pursuit for her. Best two out of three. Dobbie would pound his face in before he finished the first word.

As a last desperate measure, he decided to appeal to Libby and seek her advice. He and Libby were close and could talk about anything, though they had only ever skirted around the issue of him and Anne. She may only be sixteen, but she was wise beyond her years and would have good advice for him, he was sure. After tossing and turning for a few hours, he resolved to talk to Libby the next day and finally fell asleep.

The next morning Libby was alone in the kitchen when he entered, and he smiled as he sat down. It had been a week since the fair, and Anne hadn't spoken one word to him. He had no idea how she did it, but she had apparently gotten wise to his attempts to pin her down and outwitted him every day when he sought her out.

"Libby, I wanted to talk to you about something," he began.

She gave him a sympathetic smile and set a loaded plate in front of him. "I bet I can guess what it's about." She actually patted his head, and his smile widened. He never would have guessed he would enjoy being mothered by someone four and a half years his junior, but he did. She sat across from him and reached out her hand to him. He clasped her hand and took a deep breath.

"I don't know what to do," he started, but then the door opened and Anne and Dobbie entered. Anne pressed her lips together and looked away.

"What's going on?" Dobbie asked.

"Nothing," Libby said. "We're talking. About feelings. Want to join in?"

Dobbie plucked the clip out of her hair, and her formerly perfect French twist fell into waves down her back.

"You're tempting fate by teasing the girl who is about to feed you," she said irritably. She snatched her clip out of his fingers, re-secured her hair, and prepared plates for him and Anne.

He took off his hat, and set it on the chair beside him. "You have to be nice to me today. I might die tonight."

His plate fell in front of him with a loud clatter. "Don't joke," she said seriously.

He gave her a benevolent smile. "I thought you would be happy." His smile fled when he saw the concern on her face. "I'll be fine, Libby, it's not that big a deal."

"Then why do you have to sign a release?" she asked. "Why would they need a legal waiver clearing them of responsibility in the event of your death or dismemberment?"

He waved his hand dismissively. "That's legal mumbo jumbo. No one ever really gets hurt. Much." He grinned at her.

She turned back to the stove with a huffy sigh and a muttered, "Stubborn cowboy."

"What are you talking about?" Will asked.

"The rodeo," Dobbie said. "They're in town for a few days, and it's amateur night. It's open to anyone who wants to try his hand at it." His grin widened. "Care to give it a whirl?" he asked Will.

"No thanks. I prefer to go back to Pittsburgh in one piece."

"I'm doing it."

She said it so softly that, at first, Will wasn't sure he had heard her correctly.

"What did you say?" he asked.

"I said, I'm doing it," Anne repeated, more loudly and defiantly this time.

"Over my dead body," he said, not caring that Dobbie looked at him like he was insane.

Anne stood and smacked her palm on the table. "None of your

business, Will Ashley. My life is none of your business, and the sooner you learn that, the better off we'll both be." She threw down her napkin and practically ran out of the house.

Will debated going after her, but he heard the thundering of hooves and knew he would never be able to catch her. His horsemanship hadn't improved over the summer, and he didn't know the ranch as well as she did.

"What was that about?" Dobbie asked.

"Doesn't it concern you she's going to get herself killed?" Will asked instead.

"Yes," Dobbie said. "But once she has her mind made up, there's no stopping her. Besides, she'll be fine. She's good on the mechanical bull in Billings. It can't be much different." He returned his attention to his breakfast.

"Except these bulls have horns and hooves that can kill you," Libby said. She threw a potholder at his head and narrowly missed. Will wasn't sure if her anger was caused by her concern for him, or Anne, or both of them. She and Will shared a worried look before he excused himself and went to his room. He left his breakfast untouched, but he couldn't help it. He had lost his appetite.

By the time supper rolled around that night, he decided to appeal to her father. He hated to play the parent card, but desperate times called for desperate measures.

"Did you know Anne is thinking of competing tonight?" he asked.

"Not thinking," Anne said. "I am."

"Really?" Matt asked. His tone was more interested than concerned. He turned to study her. "Bulls or horses?"

"Bulls," she said.

"Mr. Chapman, you can't allow her to do this. Please."

"Dobbie's doing it," Matt said, as if that cleared up the argument completely.

"Dobbie is a man," Will said. Everyone put down their forks and looked at him. He held up his hands in supplication. "Fine, the truth is out; I'm a chauvinist. There are lots of things women can do as well as a man, but riding a giant, bucking bull shouldn't be one of them."

"And neither should running a ranch," Anne added. "That's what you're really trying to say, isn't it Ashley?"

"No, it's not," he said. "Not if that's what she really wants to do. But if she ends up shutting down emotionally and forcing herself to do dangerous stunts to prove she's not afraid of anything, then maybe that is what I'm saying. You can't do this, Annie."

"I can and I will," Anne said. She fled the room, and he was sure he was the only one who saw the tears in her eyes.

He turned his attention back to Matt. "Sir, please, you have to stop this insanity. She'll listen to you." In fact, Will thought she probably wanted her father or Dobbie to forbid her, if only to prove they cared.

"She's a grownup now," Matt said. "There's nothing wrong with the rodeo. Besides Dobbie, a few of the other hands are trying their luck." He plopped another helping of mashed potatoes on his plate.

Will couldn't believe his ears. When had this man stopped seeing his daughter as a woman who needed to be protected? He was sure if Libby, Kitty, or Maggie wanted to ride in the rodeo Matt would put his foot down, and that was sad. It strengthened his resolve to somehow stop Anne. She needed him to protect her because no one else would. He looked at Libby for help or advice. She shook her head at him ever so slightly, and for the second time that day he left the table without eating his food. Libby was right; it was useless to appeal to any of them for help. He would have to figure out a way to stop Anne on his own.

By the time they arrived at the rodeo that night, he thought he had found it. She and Dobbie rode together because the contestants had to be there early. He was champing at the bit to get there, and the drive to town seemed to take forever. Was Matt always such a slow driver, he wondered? Libby seemed as anxious as he was, and after a few minutes he gave up the pretense of being all right and reached out to clasp her hand. She returned his firm grip, and they held hands all the way to town. She was moving her lips silently, and he thought she might be praying.

When they arrived at the rodeo Will took off like a shot and made his way to where the entrants waited. He bypassed everyone until he saw Anne with a number pinned to her back. There was only one other girl, but she was the size and weight of most of the men, and looked like she might be able to wrestle the bull to the ground if he threw her off his back. Anne was only five foot three and probably weighed a hundred and five pounds soaking wet. He closed his eyes and swallowed hard as he caught sight of one of the massive bulls and pictured what it could do to her. Why was no one stopping this madness? Couldn't the judges of the event see what would happen to her? She was tiny and delicate. She could be crushed by one toss of the bull.

"Annie." He had to call her name a few times before she heard him. When she turned and saw him, he saw a flurry of emotions in her eyes until she pushed her face into a stubborn mask.

"Will," she said coolly. "Glad you could make it."

"Anne, you can't do this, please. Please get out of line and come sit in the stands with us. Whatever has happened between us isn't worth you risking your life over. Please."

She pressed her lips into the determined line he recognized. "I'm doing it. I can't allow you to influence the way I lead my life. I can't allow you to get inside my head and make me think and feel things I shouldn't."

"Fine," he said, "but you don't have to resolve it this way. Please. We'll talk about it. We'll come to a solution, I know we will."

"Talking is your solution to everything, but it hasn't done anything for me so far. I've talked myself to death with you, but I'm in worse shape now than when I started."

The rodeo began. She turned to look at the announcer's booth, but he caught her attention again.

"I can't allow you to do this," he said.

"What are you going to do, carry me away? Carry me out of here with my boyfriend and Dad standing a few feet away and watching?"

"No," he said, and the gravity in his tone made her give him her full attention. "I'm leaving."

"Great. Find a good seat."

"You don't understand," he said. "I can't watch you do this. If you persist in this idiocy I am leaving right now, and I'm never coming back."

That made her pause. She almost cried out, but she caught herself in time. "That's what I've been telling you to do from the beginning."

"I mean it, Anne. You do this, and it's over between us for good. I can't stand by and watch you do this to yourself."

Her lips pressed into a line again, and she crossed her arms over her chest. "Goodbye, Ashley." She didn't bat an eyelash as she watched him turn and walk away. Did he know she was only crossing her arms to hold herself together? Did he guess what was happening inside her? Now, of all times, why didn't he stay and fight for her when she needed him most? She didn't want to do this. She didn't want to ride one of those huge, scary-looking bulls, but it's what everyone expected of her. It was what she had to do. Hadn't her father and Dobbie proved that by their reaction to her decision to enter? Only Will thought it was a stupid, crazy, and reckless thing to do.

She waited in silent misery until her name was called, and then fought the urge to run away. She could do this. She was no stranger to bulls. She had some sense of how to handle them, although she also had some sense of what they were capable of. A memory of one of their ranch hands getting gored popped in her head, and she quickly shoved it away. They were prepared for accidents here. The rodeo clowns would keep the bull away from her if she was tossed off, wouldn't they? All she had to do was stay on its massive back for eight seconds. She could do anything for eight seconds.

The workers helped her onto the bull. The colossal animal was furious and breathing heavily under her legs. She could smell her fear, and she knew the bull could, too. Most likely it was adding fuel to the fire of his rage. She wrapped the rope around her gloved hand a few times and held it tightly.

"Ready?" one of the workers asked her.

She swallowed hard and nodded. *Eight seconds, eight seconds, eight seconds,* she repeated over and over.

"Cowgirl up," the worker yelled, and she could hear the amusement in his tone. Certainly it was a big joke to these professionals when a girl attempted what she was about to do.

The chute opened, and the bull stepped out into the arena. Stepped wasn't the right word. He flailed into the arena, and she was flung around like a rag doll as she attempted to cling to his back. Her bones were jarring against each other and she clamped her teeth together to keep them from chattering from the force of the impact each time the bull came back to earth.

One, she started to count the seconds in her head. It felt like an eternity. *Two,* what had she been thinking? Would this nightmare never end? *Three,* and then it did end. Before she mentally finished three she was sailing through the air and the crowd was rushing by in a blur of faces. She heard their collective gasp, and then she landed on the dirt-packed ground with a sickening thud. Her last thought was of Will. He might never know the truth because she truly believed she was about to die. She vowed that if she lived, she would tell him everything, even if she had to hunt him down to do so. Then she saw the bull advance on her, and knew she would never get the chance.

CHAPTER 23

*A*ngry voices drifted into Anne's subconscious, but she couldn't make out who they were. A girl cried, and she knew it was Libby. Or maybe it was her. Was she crying? She certainly felt like it. She had finally pushed Will away for good, and the emptiness left in his wake was crippling.

That word brought a new fear. How badly was she injured? By the smells and sounds she knew she was in the hospital, but she couldn't open her eyes. What was wrong with her?

Will, she pleaded silently, *I'm sorry. Please come back. Please give me another chance, and I'll do things right this time. Please.* The darkness of unconsciousness brought her no peace, only a restless fearfulness that wouldn't dim. It was a relief when morning came, and she could finally open her eyes.

Brilliant sunlight streamed into the room, and her eyes flew open with a purpose. She mentally ran the checklist on all her body parts and saw only her arm was broken. Her legs lifted off the bed, and she almost cried with relief. Then she did cry, but for another reason. Will was gone forever. He would never want her again, and why should he? She was broken and messed up on the inside as well as the outside now. Her arm was only a slight representation of her emotions. When her mother died she shattered into a thousand different pieces, and the intervening years had only worked to scatter the shards of her once healthy psyche.

She closed her eyes and let the tears slip gently down her face. For so long she had denied herself the luxury of releasing her tears, but Will changed all that. Since then it seemed like she hadn't been able to stop crying, and it felt oh, so good. Whoever said tears were cleansing had been correct. Finally she was able to relieve some of the pressure that had been building inside her for six years. Will had changed her world completely, and for the better. Now she would never be able to thank him. Even if she tracked him down he would never forgive her. He would return to his life where girls batted their lashes at him and vied for his attention. She pictured some pretty girl fawning over him and cried harder.

She didn't hear anyone enter her room, so when he spoke she jumped.

"Are you in pain? Can I get you something?"

Her eyes flew open. "Ashley," she said dumbly. For a second waves of joy poured over her, and then she realized his tone was cool, detached, and angry. "No, I'm fine. Thank you." They stared at each other, and she saw none of his usual warmth and affection. "I thought you were leaving."

"I was. I tried, but I couldn't go until I knew you were safe, and then when you flew off the bull I... Anyway, you're better now. I'll go." He turned, but she stopped him.

"No, please don't go."

He paused and half turned toward her again. "I have to. I'm probably fired anyway. I sort of yelled at your dad and Dobbie." He turned to go and once again she stopped him.

"No, wait," she said desperately. She *couldn't* let him leave. "You yelled at Dad and Dobbie."

He stopped again and turned to face her. He nodded.

"What did you say to them?"

"I told them they were insane to allow you to try and kill yourself on a daily basis with the things you do. I said you were a pretty show pony, but they were treating you like a draft horse. That's all I remember saying, there might have been more, but when you were unconscious I wasn't altogether with it mentally. I sort of lost it for a while."

She blinked at him. He had called her a pretty show pony? Strange how that comment felt flattering now, when before it might have sent her over the edge.

"Please don't leave me," she said softly.

"I'm not sure I have a reason to stay," he said, but his tone was soft now, too.

She patted the bed beside her. He stood debating with himself for a minute, and then he finally went over and sat beside her. She held out her hand, and he grasped it.

"I was wrong, and you were right," she said.

"About what?"

She let out a long breath. "I should have known you would never let me do this the easy way, Ashley. About everything. About us, about the rodeo, and about life in general."

"I'm afraid I'm going to need to hear the detailed version of this apology." He nestled into the bed like he was preparing for a good story. "Start at the beginning, and don't leave anything out."

She tried to pluck her hand out of his grasp, but he held firm.

"Do you know what you've put me through the last few months?" he asked. "Do you know the hoops I've jumped through for you? Do you know how little pride I have left after hearing you tease me about being what amounts to a tall girl with short hair? Do you know how many shoes I've worn through chasing you? Do you know how badly my muscles hurt after you put me in the saddle all day, or tried to beat me up numerous times?"

Her smile wouldn't stay repressed, so she grinned unrepentantly at him. "Would you have it any other way?"

"Not if it ends well," he said.

Her smile fled. "I guess that depends on your definition. Fine, here goes. You were right from the beginning. I was attracted to you the moment I saw you at the train station. You're different, but not in a bad way. I don't think you're a girl, I think you're the best man I've ever met, and I love you. I'm not in love with Dobbie, and I don't think I ever have been. I'm not some tough tomboy who can handle whatever life throws at her. I feel everything so deeply some days I don't think I'm going to make it. That day at the train depot three months ago was the first time I cried in six years, and I haven't been able to stop since, and I don't *want* to stop. Nothing has ever felt so good as setting free the person I've been trying to hide for so long, unless it's being held in your arms." She paused, but he made no move toward her. "Aren't you going to kiss me now?"

"It's your turn to kiss me," he said.

"I don't think I like this vindictive side of you, Ashley." He sat still while she sat up and slowly advanced on him. He tried to hold himself back while she kissed him, but he couldn't. He wrapped his arms around her with all the pent up emotion he'd been storing for her, and they kissed for a long time.

Finally, he withdrew and rested his forehead on hers. "You don't like ranching, do you?"

She shook her head.

"What do you want to do?"

"I," she started, stopped to gather her courage, and started again. "I want to be a lawyer. I want to prosecute criminals."

He started to laugh, and only stopped when he saw the hurt expression on her face. She had never told anyone her secret dream before, and couldn't believe he was making fun of her.

"I was picturing the criminals you're going to prosecute. They're going to be petrified of you, and you're most likely going to earn one of those nicknames like 'Bulldog.'"

"Do you really think I would be good at it, Will?"

"Maybe the best ever. I think it's what you were born to do, unless there is a job avoiding me I'm not aware of."

"I'm not avoiding you any more." Her eyes filled with tears again. "It's hopeless, though. Dad will never let me go."

Will smiled. "He will. Marie made him swear if you want to go he'll let you."

"How could you possibly know that?"

"I eavesdropped on them," Will said. "I think maybe she wanted me to hear. I think she did it for us."

She wiped her eyes with the back of her hand. "But I didn't apply to college anywhere. I'm going to have to wait a whole other semester to go somewhere, if I can even get in."

"You are really self-absorbed, you know that?" he asked.

"How does insulting me help our current situation?" she asked peevishly.

"Because you have never once asked me what my father does for a living," he said.

For a reason she didn't understand her heart began to flutter furiously. "What does your father do for a living?"

He took her hand and kissed the back of it. "He's the president of a private university in Pittsburgh. He can get you in."

"Would he? You said you and your dad don't get along well."

"Hey, you do listen to me," he said. "My dad and I might not be best friends, but my mom and I are, and he loves her. I've told her all about you, and one word from her will make him do it." He smiled, very pleased with himself.

"I can't believe this. We might actually get to be together next year," she said.

"And the year after that, and the year after that, and the year after that, and, well, you get the point."

"If you knew it was going to be this easy to work out, why didn't you tell me?" she asked.

"Why didn't I tell you? Are you crazy? I've been trying to get you to open up to me since I met you, and you…" He broke off because he realized she was teasing him. "Annie, one way or another you're going to drive me to an early grave."

"And I'll be right behind you because you're never going anywhere without me again, Will Ashley." This time she didn't need to be told to kiss him.

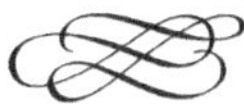

CHAPTER 24

They sat holding hands and talking about their future for a long time until her father arrived. Will gave Anne's hand a reassuring squeeze, stood, and held out his hand to the older man.

"I'm sorry I yelled at you, sir. That was disrespectful, and I apologize."

Matt Chapman nodded, and then watched Will go with a puzzled frown. He didn't understand the boy, and lately he didn't understand himself. He found himself agreeing with young Will more and more. When Will had first arrived, he mentally classified him as a sissy, but then he watched him over the summer, and his opinion changed. He wasn't afraid of anything as far as Matt could tell, least of all Anne, who had most of the other cowboys in her acquaintance running scared. Last night had proved his courage in more ways than one.

"He's a different sort of boy," Matt mused as he sat on the edge of Anne's bed.

"He is," she agreed, but her tone was much different than his. Even Matt couldn't overlook the almost dreamlike way she spoke.

"What about Dobbie?" he asked. He loved Dobbie like his own son, and the marriage between him and Anne was something he had long anticipated. Besides the fact he loved the young man, it made good business sense.

"I don't love Dobbie, Dad," Anne said, and she started to cry.

Matt scowled and cast about for something to do or say. Times like these were when he missed his Claire the most. She always knew what to do in every situation, especially ones where emotions were involved. He had grown comfortable in his relationship with Anne because he thought she was stoic, like him, but here she was blubbering all over the place, and he realized for the second time in two days that he hadn't done right by her. Marie was right; Claire would not be pleased with his lack of parenting their little girls. At least he could ask her what was wrong; that was a good starting point.

"What is it, little girl?"

To his consternation she cried harder, and threw herself into his embrace. It had been so long since he held her like this that he had forgotten the rush of emotions that always swelled inside him, along with a million memories. The first time he found out it was a girl and Claire told him he wouldn't be sad it wasn't a boy once he saw his little daughter. The first time he held her and had to tell Claire she was right. The first time she had called him Daddy. The first time he put her on a horse and she squealed with delight. When was the last time Anne had seemed delighted over anything? When was the last time he had hugged her? How had he fooled himself into believing she was a capable adult who could handle anything a man could when, in reality, she was still a little girl who needed him?

For a long time he held her, and it felt like medicine. It filled an ache inside him he hadn't realized he had, and then she spoke, shattering the peaceful moment.

"I don't want to be foreman anymore, Dad," she said. She pulled away to look at him, and her eyes brimmed with tears as she waited his answer.

At first he didn't say anything. He couldn't. Out of all of his daughters, Anne was the one who was closest to the child of his dreams. Claire used to say she was the son he never had. He knew the other girls would most likely drift away from the ranch, but he thought

Anne was cut out for the life. She was good at it, as good as him, or maybe even better. He had visions of her and Dobbie's children some day taking over and continuing what his great-great-grandfather had started. He was the first Chapman in generations not to produce a son, but he didn't mind because he had Anne. And now she was telling him she didn't want it. He almost raised his voice to tell her she had no choice in the matter, and she would stay whether she wanted to or not. Then he remembered Marie.

His dratted sister had been right again. How did women know the things they did? At the time he promised her the girls could leave if they wanted he had thought she was talking about Kitty. With her intellect, he knew she would most likely go to one of those ivy-league colleges on the east coast. If he knew he was making the promise about Anne, he probably wouldn't have done it.

"What do you want?" he asked.

"I want to go to Pittsburgh with Will. I want to go to college there and become a lawyer, but not the bad kind. The good kind that prosecutes criminals."

He had to smile at that. He had never been shy with his opinions, especially those concerning politicians and lawyers.

"Sounds like you've given it a lot of thought," he said. "You don't like the ranch."

"Dad," she said, and her eyes filled with tears again. "I love the ranch. I love the beauty, and the smells, and the sounds. I'll miss it every day I'm away." She averted her eyes. "But I won't miss inseminating the cows, and having to put down injured heifers, and horses, and dogs, and trying to budget feed for the animals, and lots of other things like that."

He should have known better than to put all that weight on her little shoulders. He hadn't done it intentionally. After Claire's death, he had been out of his head. Anne had picked up the slack, and she did so well with it he never took it back again. In his mind making her foreman was a great honor. To her it had been detrimental.

"Don't look like that, Dad," she said. "I know what you're thinking. I haven't been miserable, and I'm not scarred for life. I want the chance to make my own way and do something different. Who knows, maybe I'll hate being a lawyer and come back to the ranch some day."

He nodded and put on a happy face. A part of him was happy for her, and proud of her. She was an independent little cuss, and she had initiative and ambition. Claire would have been proud of her, too. She had given him six years of her life. That was longer than he had ever had a foreman before, and to try and keep her any longer was unfair.

"All right, little girl. You can go to Pittsburgh with your young man, but you're going to have to tell Dobbie."

Her second of joy quickly fled. "I don't want to hurt him. I never wanted that. He's like a brother to me."

"He's reasonable and level headed. I'm sure with time he'll move on and be fine." Matt wouldn't allow himself to think of what might happen if that weren't true.

Anne nodded, but she didn't look convinced.

"Did you know Will jumped into the arena last night?" her father asked.

Anne's head jerked up. "He did what?"

"When the bull tossed you and started to charge, he jumped the fence and ran straight at it to distract it. *He* almost got trampled, but then the rodeo clowns intervened at the last minute."

She remembered her last moment of consciousness when the bull was descending on her. Will had placed himself in harm's way to save her and almost gotten himself killed because of her foolish need to prove herself.

"He told me he yelled at you," she said.

"He did. I thought he might take a swing at me. I was sort of hoping he would. I think I deserved it for letting you go into that arena." He thought of the previous night when Will had been so upset. At the time he had been too distracted by his own worry to notice the contrast between him and Dobbie. Dobbie was worried, no doubt about that, but he seemed more focused on trying to calm Libby's weeping. Will had been the one who was nearly undone, until the doctor told them Anne was all right. He fought the urge to shake his head. That was the sort of thing his wife would have picked up on. He wondered if he would ever stop missing and needing her. In a rare moment of romanticism, he studied his oldest daughter. Was that the kind of love she and young Ashley had found? For her sake he hoped so. There was nothing like it, and the possibility that she had somehow made the pain of losing her lessen.

"Tell me all about what's been going on behind my back with you and our tutor," he said. He leaned forward and listened as she told him rapturously of the secret summer she had been having right under his nose.

CHAPTER 25

*E*verything happened quickly after that day in the hospital. Anne, Will, and her father returned home. Will carried her bags to her room while Libby fussed over her and tried to fix her food. Dobbie popped his head in to ask if she was all right, and frowned when she told him she wanted to see him in the barn. She had never dreaded anything more than what she was about to do.

As they walked side by side to the barn she thought of all the many times they had done so over the years. There was an ocean of memories between them, and if not for Will, she would have called the whole thing off and gone through with her relationship with Dobbie. But now she couldn't. Now she knew what she was missing, and a sweet and pleasant friendship wasn't enough. She needed the passionate connection she and Will shared.

"What is it, Anne?" Dobbie asked impatiently when they reached the barn. Emotions made him jittery, and he could sense she was getting ready to talk about her feelings.

Anne was usually straightforward, but she was having trouble saying what she wanted to say. She picked at a loose nail and studied it while she attempted to speak.

"You know you're my best friend," she said. She glanced at him, saw that he nodded, and resumed picking at the nail. "Besides Libby, there's always been you in my life to count on. We've spent lots of time together over all our lives. We have things in common. We're a lot alike in all the ways that count, and I love you."

They had never said that to each other before, and he didn't like that she was the one who said it first. It made him feel odd somehow.

She sensed his irritation and hurried on. "The problem is that I love you like a brother, and not like I should if we're talking marriage. I'm not in love with you. I'm in love with Will, and I'm leaving with him and going to Pittsburgh."

He stared at her, sure he had misheard. She was leaving the ranch? She was leaving him for another man? She was breaking up with him after four years, just like that? What about the future they had planned? What about all they had built together, and dreamed of building?

"You've been sneaking around behind my back with that city guy?" he asked incredulously. All he thought he knew about her was crumbling at his feet. The Anne he knew would never cheat on him.

Her eyes filled with tears. "Yes," she whispered, and then she started to cry.

Her tears were more shocking than her confession. He never in all their lives ever remembered seeing her cry. "You cheated on me, you're dumping me, and you're shirking your responsibilities here."

She swallowed hard and nodded, but she was no longer able to look at him. "I'm sorry. I treated you horribly, and you deserved better. I never guessed I would behave so dishonorably, but I couldn't help falling in love with him."

He stared at her for another minute. He had nothing more to say to her, but he was too shocked to walk away. A million thoughts ran through his head, but he didn't know how to express them. That had always been their problem, he realized. They didn't know how to talk to each other. Finally, when he could take it no more, he turned and walked away.

She wanted to call to him, but what could she say? She had already told him she was sorry, and she meant it, but that didn't make things better. She couldn't tell him she would forget the whole thing and stay with him because she wouldn't mean that, either. As much as she hated to hurt him, she wanted to be with Will, and she wanted to go away.

When Will found her in the hayloft a short time later, she wasn't surprised. What was a surprise was how easy it was to fall into his embrace and let him comfort her now. It was like heaven to finally stop fighting him and give in to her need of him.

"I'm sorry," he said gently. "I'm so sorry you're hurting. I would do anything to take it away."

"Hold me," she said.

"For the rest of our lives," he answered. They stayed that way for a couple more hours, and then they went inside.

Dobbie didn't come to supper that night, and her sisters looked around the table in dismay.

"Where's Dobbie?" Maggie asked. "Is he sick?"

Anne cleared her throat. Since she spent the afternoon crying in the hayloft she hadn't yet told them of her decision.

"Dobbie and I broke up."

Her father and Will kept eating, but the three other forks clattered onto the table.

"Why?" Maggie asked.

"Because Will and I are together now."

Kitty, Maggie, and Libby looked at Will. Maggie was in shock, but Kitty and Libby weren't. Kitty looked slightly bored by the proclamation, and Libby looked happy. Although, she was clearly worried about Dobbie and kept turning to look out the door for him.

"You and Will are boyfriend and girlfriend?" Maggie asked.

"Yes," Anne said, and to Will's amusement she blushed. That did shock Kitty and Libby. They didn't know their sister was capable of such a girlish action.

"Is Will going to move in here?" Maggie asked hopefully.

Kitty and Libby leaned in to hear the answer.

"No," Anne said. "I'm going away to Pittsburgh with him."

They stared at her. "You're…going…away," Libby said slowly. She stared unfocused at a spot between them.

Maggie started to cry. "No. No, you can't go away. You can both stay here. Will can have my pony if the other horses are too scary for him." She put her hands over her face. Libby started to pull her into her embrace, but Anne beat her to it, and everyone looked at her in astonishment again. She was usually the one telling them to buck up.

"It's all right, sweetie," she said gently. "We'll talk on the phone all the time. You can take care of my horse for me. No one will do it better than you."

That stopped Maggie's tears. "Can I ride her sometimes?"

"As much as you want," Anne said. "She'll be sad and lonely with no one to ride her."

Maggie picked up her fork again and started to eat, but Kitty and Libby remained fixed on Anne's face in surprise.

"You're going away," Libby said again. In all her romantic dreams for Will and Anne, she never thought her sister would leave. She had no idea Anne even wanted to go. She had thought they would date long distance for a couple of years, and then Will would return when he graduated college.

"I am, Lib," Anne said. "I'm sorry I didn't tell you sooner, but we only figured it out today."

Libby nodded and took a dish to the stove for a refill. Anne and Will both knew she was hiding tears and stared at her back in concern. In all their happy preparation, they hadn't considered what would happen to Libby. She and Anne were best friends, and the ranch was so isolated they only had each other. Now Anne would be off having adventures while Libby was still chained to her kitchen. Will sneaked his hand under the table and gave Anne's a reassuring squeeze. When Libby turned back around she was smiling, and it looked mostly genuine.

The next few days passed in a blur of packing and preparation. They had decided to go to Pittsburgh early so Anne could fill out the necessary paperwork. She had already faxed her application and been rushed through the acceptance process, thanks to Will's father. She was glad she took the SAT, even though at the time she never imagined what she would need it for. Maybe some premonition about her future had kept hope alive.

Her sisters finally recovered from their shock over her departure, only to have a greater shock on the day she left. Anne was crying. None of them but Libby could ever remember her crying over anything, ever. Now she wasn't crying; she was sobbing. She held each of them for a long, long time and sobbed until their shirts were wet and they ended up comforting her. She repeated the same scene with her father, and then gave a wistful look to the bunkhouse.

She had already said her goodbyes to her men, but Dobbie remained invisible. She supposed he worked, but no one had seen him since the scene in the barn. He hadn't come to supper. Anne prayed he would be all right and she hadn't caused him any permanent damage. Surely he would soon realize how shallow their relationship had been. He would move on. He would find someone of his own.

Still, she felt guilty. Will knew, and put his arm around her when they boarded the train.

"It's time for me to tell you a secret I've been keeping all summer," he said.

She dried her eyes and perked up. "What is it?"

"It's about Dobbie and Libby."

"What about Dobbie and Libby?"

"Don't you think it's odd how they're both the nicest people in the world, yet when they're near each other they fight constantly?"

"That's their way," Anne said.

"That's their way because they're in love with each other, and neither of them knows it."

Her mouth dropped open, and she stared at him. "No way. They would kill each other."

"Wait and see," he said smugly.

She turned to look out the window and puzzle over the suggestion. He was usually right about these things. Dobbie and Libby. She smiled. She never would have guessed.

*L*ibby stood at the sink and stared listlessly at her garden. She needed to weed, water, harvest, can, clean, do laundry, iron, bake, and make supper, but instead she stayed rooted to her spot.

If she knew things were going to change so drastically, would she still have wanted Will and Anne to get together? That was a difficult question to answer, and the fact that she paused over it filled her with guilt. Why wouldn't she want what was best for two people she loved dearly? The only answer was purely selfish. She didn't want her world to change. She didn't want her sister to leave. They had only been gone a day, and she was already sad and lonely without them. For the past six years she and Anne had been a team as they worked together to keep their family afloat. Now she was alone, completely and utterly alone.

On top of all that, she was worried about Dobbie. No one had seen or heard from him since the day of Anne's return from the hospital. Libby set a heaping plate of food outside his door for every meal, and they always came back clean the next morning, so she knew at least he was eating. She wished he would walk through the door and tease her. Then she would know everything was back to normal and he was okay. They were his only family, and the thought that one of them had caused him pain was excruciating to her. She should have forced Anne to break up with him when it became apparent she and Will were getting together. Why didn't she? It might have saved him some hurt.

The door banged behind her and she turned, hoping it might be Dobbie and she could provoke him out of his blue mood. It wasn't Dobbie, though, it was Maggie.

"He's gone," Maggie blurted.

"What?" Libby said, although the way her heart sank to her toes forewarned her of her sister's meaning.

"Dobbie's gone," Maggie said.

"I'm sure he's in one of the far pastures somewhere," Libby said, and swallowed hard. Yes, that had to be it.

"No, Rook said his room is completely cleared out. He's gone, really, really gone." Tears sprang to her eyes and stuck there as a most unusual thing happened. Libby burst into tears, sank to the floor, and put her hands over her face. In her shock Maggie forgot her own tears. Instead she went forward and, for the first time in her young life, acted as the caregiver to her older sister as she cradled Libby close and tried to dry her eyes.

*T*hank you for reading *The Cowgirl Code*, the first book in the Queens of Montana Series. For more books, please check out my website at www.vanessagraybartal.com